ANCÓN

A NOVEL BY
JOHN S. MASSEY

authorHOUSE®

AuthorHouse™
1663 Liberty Drive
Bloomington, IN 47403
www.authorhouse.com
Phone: 1-800-839-8640

Published by AuthorHouse   12/23/2014

ISBN: 978-1-4969-6136-5 (sc)
ISBN: 978-1-4969-6135-8 (e)

Library of Congress Control Number: 2014922692

Any people depicted in stock imagery provided by Thinkstock are models,
and such images are being used for illustrative purposes only.
Certain stock imagery © Thinkstock.

This book is printed on acid-free paper.

Because of the dynamic nature of the Internet, any web addresses or
links contained in this book may have changed since publication and
may no longer be valid. The views expressed in this work are solely those
of the author and do not necessarily reflect the views of the publisher,
and the publisher hereby disclaims any responsibility for them.

Contents

DEDICATION

I dedicate this book to my very best friend and business partner, Wilbert. He taught me all about Peru, and after so many trips to this amazing country, gave me the love for its culture, people, food, and mysteries that inspired this story. Also to the Inca people and their complex civilization, who were inspirational in sharing just a little piece of their amazing culture and art.

Disclaimer

This is an original work of fiction. All characters appearing in this work are fictitious. Any resemblance to real persons, living or dead, is purely coincidental. Resemblances to actual international companies that indulge in GMO research, sales, profits, and human misery may be possible....

Prologue - Inchi

Among the many native South American people, there are many legends, mostly passed from generation to generation through the oral tradition. One of the central themes in many of such legends is the corn plant, which was revered as one of the first foods since time began. After Mother Nature, was the corn mother, or Pachamama who was the spiritual mother of all families. Pachamama was also a jealous mother, and vowed to return to reclaim the land and her people in the fifth, and final world, when it was rumored, that the corn plant would be corrupted and made useless.

He studied the quipu, with its knots and colors, and "read" the prophecy written by the Incas so long ago. It had to be translated into narrative from a series of glyphs that had taken decades of research and study to decode. Literally, it read something to the effect of, "When the peoples of the fifth world arrive, there will be great pain from the second mother, Inchi. She will bear many children and become like the sunlight, and rivers of yellow will fill the world. The birds and the animals will drink of the river and multiply in great abundance, and the people of the fifth world will multiply as well. There will be both joy and then great sorrow as demons plunder the land, and many will die. Pachamama will reach through the former worlds and seize back her broken sons and daughters, and a great calamity will destroy the fifth world. And it will be made new."

Bernardo stared at the label on the tightly sealed vial, *Escherichia coli 0157,H7*. It had just killed fifteen children and a 60-year-old woman in Lima, Peru. It was a bacterium that was resistant to acid, specifically stomach acid, and all known antibiotics, and caused renal failure within 24 hours of ingestion. *Mother Inchi…* he thought to himself, and slipped the vial into the airtight container. Corn, chicha, cancha, maize, zea mays; the twenty-first-century weapon that had killed his wife. Number 2 field corn, the commodity that was threatening to destroy his country. He turned a figurine of a small golden condor in his fingers and burned with revenge. Wait, Pachamama. Stay your hand just a while longer…

CHAPTER ONE - BERNARDO

1957

Bernardo chewed mindlessly on his ceviche, sitting on the docks looking out over the Bay of Ancón. The fish was still fresh, but soon it would be closing time for the restaurant, even though it was only three forty-five in the afternoon. It was still traditional, after all these years, to not offer ceviche after four o'clock. It would not be fresh enough. The locals knew this, but the tourists; ah, that was another story entirely. They always complained that the restaurants closed too early. Now there was less and less complaining due to the lack of tourists. Ancón had become, for all intents and purposes, a ghost town.

He gazed at the water as the sun was setting. Fishing boats were bobbing up and down gently in the water off the pier. Fall had come upon his country, and the light faded quickly in the late afternoon, throwing long shadows along the boardwalk. He sighed to himself, as he imagined the ghosts of crowds that used to promenade up and down the finely decorated boulevard with its swirling patterns of black and white terrazzo. Gone.

The old boulevard wound past the old homes and the old hotel where he'd stayed with his family as a young boy; all old now, just like him. Inevitably, he found his thoughts turning to his Emelia, and the events of the last few days and this afternoon. He had come to take her ashes to this small seaside town that time and the rich and famous had long forgotten. He planned to dump her remains unceremoniously into the harbor of the city they had lived in and loved in for so long. He sighed deeply and picked at his food without appetite. Sadness swept over him in rip-current waves, threatening to pull him out to sea and drown him, but the tears would not come. Not anymore. All he felt was a numb emptiness that can only come from prolonged grieving and great loss. There was nothing left for him now but bitterness. The only love of his life was no longer by his side. He placed his fork gently on the plate, motioned for the waiter to come, paid the 50 soles, and left for his room in the old hotel.

Walking back to the hotel, he gazed up the hills to the brown desert above, surrounding the entire village. Not a sign of green anywhere. Hidden far within the hills was his spacious hacienda, which he had chosen not to stay in. He wanted total privacy and anonymity. It was still hard to imagine how this jewel north of Lima had ever come into being. By all rights, it should have been just a continuation of the desolate landscape. But throughout its checkered history, Ancón was the landing place of the invading Chilean Army in 1880 and in 1883. It was the meeting place of the Chilean and Peruvian commissioners who had drawn up the Treaty of Ancón, which ended the bloody war between Chile and Peru. The war may have ended officially then, but there was still a deep mistrust, if not hatred, of the Chileans to this day.

In its day, in the late nineteenth and early twentieth centuries, Ancón was a deluxe, upscale beach resort, whose sandy soil and dry climate made it a welcome place for persons with pulmonary and bronchial afflictions. It also held a few other secrets from much longer ago.

***

Bernardo Jorge Fuento Villacorta was born in Lima, Peru on January 21, 1947. His father, Raphael, and mother, Alejandra, lived in a comfortable home in Miraflores, on Pradier-Fodere. He had one younger sister, Gabina, and an older brother, Lotario. Papi was an accountant, and worked long hours to support his family. It was an exciting time to be living in Lima, the "City of the Kings." The Presidential Palace was being re-built downtown, and was constructed over a huge Indian burial ground called Waka that had a shrine of the Indian chief Taulichusco. The main architect, Ricardo de Jaxa Malachowski, was a friend of Raphael's. They'd met when Ricardo had first moved to Peru in 1911. That was so typical of Peru; it was a giant European melting pot. Malachowski himself was of Polish and Slovak origins. Papi and Ricardo arranged to work together on many projects, but this one, the Presidential Palace, was perhaps his most ambitious yet. He needed a trusted friend to keep the books and monitor the finances.

For many of those years, the family would spend December and January in Ancón, an easy trip on the old Lima-Ancón-Chancay Railway. The Chancay portion was apparently lost in 1879 during the war with the Chileans. To the children, it was magical 42-kilometer trip through the vast deserts surrounding Lima. There was almost always a prevailing mist, *la niebla*, which hung over the coast, giving an even more ethereal feeling to the pilgrimage. Bernardo didn't remember much of these trips until the summer of '57, when he was barely ten and a half years old. Mama would usually take the children on ahead, and Papi would join them later in the week after working in Lima. Ancón was alive with fishermen and tourists, boats and bathing suits, and most of all—La Playa. Their house was only a block from the water, and his brother and sister and Bernardo spent all day either in the water, or playing on the beach. Mama would escort them there with Angelina, their maid, and then stroll up and down the boulevard, talking with friends and having coffee with the locals, who had come to know her well over the years.

It was on such a day—a Saturday, as he remembered, because Papi was with them at the beach—that Bernardo first felt the pain of love. He had been told for many years later that a ten-and-a-half-year-old was not capable of such things, but he knew it to be true, even to this day. Down the beach, long brown hair flowing behind her, running with a kite in the wind, was a beautiful young girl. Her kite was clearly not functioning well. The tail was much too short, so it kept crashing into the beach over and over. And although she would gleefully pick it up and run with two other girls down the beach, who turned out to be her sisters, the kite would continue to crash headfirst into the sand.

"It's too short!" he yelled to her.

The girls stopped and turned, looking directly at Bernardo with fire in their eyes. Who was this ridiculous boy shouting at them? He walked towards the prettiest one and her sisters, pointing at the kite.

"The tail's too short; it will never fly like that," he said, with the most authority he could muster. The girls laughed, all except for the oldest one. The fire was still in her eyes.

"And who are you to tell me about my kite, little boy? Go away!" She flipped her hair to the side and turned her back on him.

He was crushed. "Please," he ran after her, "I meant no harm. I think if we could just find a scrap of cloth to add to the tail, your kite would soar like the wind!"

She turned to him, eyes still flashing. "And where would I get such a piece of cloth, hmm?"

In his haste to solve the problem, and, of course get to speak with this enchanting girl, it had never occurred to Bernardo where he might find the solution to the problem tail. His eyes searched the beach, up and down, looking for something, anything that would become the salvation of the kite and the deliverer of his dignity. In desperation, he seized on a solution so reckless; he knew he would not only have Mama furious with him, but also perhaps the further humiliation of having his plan backfire on him as well.

"Wait, just one moment, please," he beckoned to her, and sprinted back to his towel as fast as he had ever run before.

Grabbing the towel in his teeth, he tore a strip off the side, dropped the rest, and ran twice as fast back to Emelia and her sisters, all who clearly looked as if he had taken leave of his senses. "Here," he said, breathing so hard from running he thought he would explode. "This should do."

The girl lifted one eyebrow with an air of skepticism, but gestured towards the injured kite. "Well, go ahead, Señor Ingeniero," she said with a slight grin. "Make it work." The girls giggled. His hands trembled as he tied the piece of towel to the end of the kite, but he tied it firmly.

"All right," he said. "Let's give it a try." Almost as if on cue, a slight breeze blew in from the harbor, and he encouraged her to run down the beach again.

"Go on!" he said. "Try it! Run!"

And with that, the beautiful, brown-haired girl straightened the line, gripped it firmly in her hand, and sprinted down the beach. The kite shot up into the sky, then wobbled slightly to the left, then the right. "Let out some line!" he shouted to her. She let the line slide through her fingers. Up and up the kite began to soar. They all started yelling and laughing. The kite was now in flight by itself, high above the harbor with the pelicans.

He came to her side, smiling. "I'm Bernardo," he said, extending his hand. She looked at his hand, and then looked at the kite, and then looked into his eyes, and smiled.

"I'm Emelia," she said. She shook his hand firmly. "Pleased to meet you, Bernardo, Señor Ingeniero," she said, and laughed. "Here, you take this; I have to go now." She handed him the string. Before he could say another word, she ran to her two sisters and they sprinted down the beach, across the boardwalk, and disappeared down a side street.

He never even had time to say, "Wait!" What had just happened? He felt a knot forming in his stomach.

He went back his brother and sister and they laughed at him. Lotario said, "You should see your face, Papi! You look as if you saw the Madonna herself!" He burst into laughter.

Bernardo handed his brother the kite string. "Here. Take this," he said through clenched teeth. He was so humiliated.

Bernardo stooped down to the sand and snatched up what was left of his towel, then stormed off to their apartment. All the way home he scanned the streets and boulevard for this new, exotic creature, Emelia. Nothing. He was desperate to find where she had gone. She had simply vanished. He kept playing the beach scene out in his head, over and over again;

her hair in the wind, her eyes, the kite, her touch. He didn't know what was wrong with him. He had this deepening ache in his stomach, and his throat felt dry and tight. He thought he was getting sick. When he arrived home, Mama was both surprised and angry, especially when she saw the torn towel.

"Back so soon? What is this?" she exclaimed, shaking the towel in his face. The Villacortas were a wealthy family by most Peruvian standards, but Mama was very frugal. She made things last. The towel had been purchased for their vacation. He stammered out his explanation as he watched her eyes get wider, and then a smile crept across her face.

"Oh, Papi, this is so cute! You did this to help a little girl? How sweet you are!" She hugged him and told him to try to use older towels when he was rescuing girls in the future. His mother had a wonderful way of putting things into their proper perspective. She always took things in stride. He never loved her more than that day.

"But, Mama," he said, "I'm not feeling well. I think I may be sick."

She felt his forehead, and told him with a smile to go upstairs and lie down. "There is nothing wrong with you, Papi," she said, as she hugged him close. "You're just lovesick."

He had no understanding of what she meant, but went upstairs and fell fast asleep in his bed. His sister woke him up for supper. He was not hungry, but forced himself out of bed and into the kitchen, where the family was assembled for dinner. Mama's meals were usually prepared by Angelina, and therefore edible. While Mama was wonderful in many ways, the Lord had not blessed her with the gift of cooking. And why should she have learned? She herself was brought up in the nobility of Lima, never having to lift a hand for anything. She called us all to prayer and eyed Papa with "the look" which meant, "Go ahead, you're the head of the household…pray!" And so Papa prayed a quick prayer, thanking Jesus, the Virgin Mary, and all the saints for our good fortune and good food.

"Amen!" we all exclaimed, and passed bowls of food around. There was always lively discussion at supper, but tonight, Bernardo was the subject of much more than he wanted to be.

Gabina, who was six, began. "Mama, did Bernardo tell you about his new *girlfriend*?" She started giggling uncontrollably.

Before Mama could even answer, his brother, who was 12, tattled, "Oh, yes, Papa, Bernardo is a great *ingeniero* now.

(Laughter around the table.) "He redesigns kites for little girls in distress!" And they exploded with laughter again.

Papa, trying to keep a stern face, said to Bernardo, "Yes, your mother told me that you fixed that little girl's kite on the beach this afternoon. That was a nice thing to do, Papi."

He stared sternly at his daughter and son. Bernardo felt the warmth of embarrassment creeping up his neck.

Mama broke in, "I think it's sweet that you have found a new friend, Papi. Don't let this silly sister and this ill-mannered brother of yours spoil your feelings, or your dinner. Now eat!"

He picked at his food. Thoughts of the brown-haired girl Emelia were swimming in his mind. The conversation settled onto Papa's work at the Presidential Palace. Then more jokes about Bernardo getting married soon, where the wedding would be…he felt sick. He could not eat, nor endure any more ridicule. He threw his napkin down and ran to his room, humiliated and embarrassed.

He could hear his mother yelling at his brother and sister all the way from the top of the stairs. "Now see what you've done! Leave your brother alone! He is so sensitive! Stop it, now!"

As he lay in his bed that night, he resolved that first thing in the morning he was going to march down to the beach and find that girl. He had so many questions; where did she live? What was her family like? When would he see her again? Did she come to the beach every day? He fell asleep, but it was a restless evening, tossing and turning, mostly spent waiting for the sun to come up.

Chapter Two

Present Day

A knock on the door startled Bernardo awake. He looked at his watch; barely daylight at seven thirty in the morning. He struggled out of bed and shuffled to the door.

"Who is it?" he whispered, still half-asleep.

"National Police, señor," a crisp voice responded. "We have urgent business for you to attend to back in Lima. Please, señor, get dressed and come with us quickly!" The voice left no room for protest or negotiation. It was firm. Bernardo cracked the door open slightly, wearing only his underwear, and peered into the hallway. There were three men, dressed in typical police uniforms, machine guns at the ready. They were all very fit, and all business. "I apologize for the hour, señor. We have our orders."

"Very well," muttered Bernardo, looking the man who had knocked on his door squarely in the eyes. "Let me get dressed and gather up my things. I'll be outside in fifteen minutes."

"I apologize, Señor Villacorta," said the stocky, well-built officer. "But I must remain here with you outside your door until you're ready to leave; for your safety, señor. My men will escort us to our vehicle outside when you're ready."

"Very well," he muttered. "I'll be just a moment."

He shut the door, removed his old underwear and replaced them with a fresh pair. Then he shuffled to the bathroom to splash cold water over his face and wash the sleep from his eyes. He grabbed a toothbrush and shoved it in his mouth, brushing with one hand while he struggled to put on his shirt and pants that were hanging on a nearby hook with the other. Hopping around the room, he finally abandoned the toothbrush on the bed. He pulled up his pants and thought to himself, *when did putting my pants on get to be so difficult?* He reached for socks and laced up his shoes. He glanced around the room. Where had he left his laptop and briefcase? It was by the window on his favorite old desk, overlooking the harbor. He began shoving papers and the laptop into the briefcase, pulling the plug for the computer out of the wall and stuffing that in another compartment.

"Señor, por favor!" the voice outside his door said loudly this time. "We must go now!"

"All right, all right, I'm coming," he said, struggling with his jacket. He opened the door and was immediately saluted by the man who had been so insistent, heels snapping together accompanying the salute.

"Please, señor, come this way." Bernardo noticed as they walked that his escorts' eyes constantly moved around the hallway and up and down the stairway. They exited through the back entry, next to the kitchen, where a large black Mercedes E 300 AMG was parked, engine running. The driver jumped out of the car and ran around to the rear passenger door, opened it, and snapped to full attention. Bernardo got in. The other men took offensive positions, two in front and one on the other side of Bernardo in the rear. They sped off, heading for the Pan-American Highway back towards Lima. Not a word was said, nor were any needed.

Bernardo had left town with his beloved Emelia's ashes without saying a word to anyone, least of all his business partners. He had earned the right to a few days of privacy. Other than an occasional day off due to national holidays, he had hardly done anything but work and travel for the past…how long had it been? There was other business that needed attention in Ancón, but it clearly would have to wait, at least for the time being. Bernardo made a mental note to complete this other business at another time, but soon. Little did he know how important that other business would turn out to be.

The car sped down the Pan-American at high speed until they reached the outskirts of Lima. Even at this early hour, heavy traffic was already slowing everything to a crawl. "*Mierda!*" the officer cursed quietly under his breath, and leaned forward to flip a switch under the dashboard. Blue blinking lights lit up under the front grillwork, and in the rear of the car as well. A siren began wailing, and slowly the traffic parted, as if it were the Red Sea itself. The driver sped up, artfully weaving in and out and around other cars and buses in the early morning traffic. It was a dance of sorts. Bernardo was always surprised at the lack of accidents in this intricate ballet on the streets of Lima. To the untrained eye, it looked like a free-for-all; cars speeding up and then braking at the last moment, barely missing each other, cutting across lanes of traffic with seeming disregard for human life. In all his years in this city, he had only witnessed one accident, and it involved more yelling and screaming about broken taillights and injured grills and personalities than any physical damage.

As the car closed in on the center of the city, the driver began to take alternate routes, weaving back and forth on one-way streets, circling ever closer to the familiar destination he had spent so much of his adult life in, and the very place where his own father had made his first fortune: Palacio de Gobierno, the Presidential Palace. There was a back driveway; high gates topped with ribbon wire and two heavily armed National Police guards, H&K MP5 9mm machine guns at the ready. The gates opened, but the guards hardly changed their forward stares, acknowledging the vehicle and its contents. Business as usual. Instead of pulling to the side entrance, the car continued to a ramp that led downward, inside the palace. The dimly lit, cobblestoned tunnel led further downward, curving slightly to the right. Down and down it went for another three hundred meters into the bowels of the city. Brighter lights approached, and the car stopped in a landing area, a portico carved out of stone. The three security guards jumped out, one opening the door for Bernardo.

"Thank you," he muttered at the young, brown face. The guard nodded his head slightly, motioning towards the riveted steel door on the far wall near the rear of the car.

Another guard had already begun to open the door. Bright light spilled out towards the car, and the entrance greeted him with elegant oriental rugs on heavy stone floors. *The familiar halls of the inner circles of power in the country,* he thought to himself. He walked a few meters to one of twenty ornately decorated heavy wooden doors. The artistry of each door was different, depicting detailed scenes of the history of his beloved country. The Nazca door, as this one was called, had detailed characters of what the ancient ones had inscribed on the land so long ago: the spider, hummingbirds, monkeys, fish, sharks or orcas, llamas, and lizards. They had jewels for eyes, and were embossed with gold and silver. They were truly works of art, each of them.

He entered the lavishly decorated room, with its overstuffed leather furniture and large tables. Flowers and fruit were everywhere. A large table to the right was set with a starched white linen tablecloth and a fine silver coffee pot, sugar, creamer, and spoons, alongside bone china cups and saucers. There was fresh, warm bread, and cheese on a platter. Slices of several types of meat and sausages and bowls of black olives sat in other silver dishes.

"We need to talk," a voice to his left said. He turned and saw the familiar drab olive uniform of his trusted friend and confidante for over four decades, General Victor de la Hoya. Bernardo knew full well that this had to have been important for the meeting to occur in this manner and in this place. He knew better than to show impatience, or anything but respect.

"Victor, my old friend, I'm at your service, of course," he said with a slight bow, and extended his hands. They hugged and kissed each other on the cheeks and pushed back.

"Coffee? Something to eat, perhaps, after your ride into the city?" The general waved at the table of food and drink.

"Just coffee, thank you," Bernardo replied. "I don't have much of an appetite these days." He walked to the table and poured himself some hot, black coffee.

"Ah, yes, of course…Emelia." The general looked down at the floor. "I know any words I may say at this time will not suffice, so I'll only say that I'm so very sorry for your loss. I loved her as a member of my own family."

"Thank you, Victor," Bernardo uttered in a quiet voice.

"Please," the general continued, as he gestured towards two large stuffed chairs separated by a small reading table. "Let us sit and talk." They both sat down crisply in their respective chairs.

This was an unusually formal meeting, considering the depth of their friendship. It had to be a subject of great significance. There was also an excellent chance that the meeting was being monitored, or actually watched by others.

The general got right to the point. "There are two reasons we need to have a discussion: One of our most trusted brothers turned up dead last night. It was Montoya. He was murdered. Shot twice in the back of the head with a small caliber weapon; his hands were tied behind his back. He was found on Jose Prado late in the evening. The police have questioned many people, but of course no one saw anything. We're still investigating. Unfortunately," he continued, "there was also a note. Perhaps it might better be called a warning, a threat. I can't really say. It was typed with some old-style typewriter; you know, the kind we all used to use?"

Bernardo nodded, mind spinning. He was stunned at the news, but said nothing.

The general paused as if he was about to utter something very grave. "The note was a partial list of names; some first names, some last names, but no complete names, plus many numbers and letters. To any of us, they might as well have been complete names; I knew whom the list spoke of immediately, but was puzzled by the numbers, 34H31 and 33P67, to name but two. There were probably more than twenty in all. To others, it would have appeared like a list of gibberish, random names, like a crazy person might write. At the end of list, there were three words, *Traidores de oro*. Here it is. What do you make of it?" He slid the dirty scrap of paper over the table to Bernardo. Attached to the piece of paper was a cotton thread with a series of knots in it.

"This looks almost like a tiny quipu, does it not?" Bernardo examined the string closely.

The general nodded. "We made up a copy of it for you, with the string duplicated as well as we could make out. I'll give you this copy to study." The general slid a larger copy of the scrap of paper towards Bernardo, who then mindlessly slipped it into his pocket.

Bernardo knew Miguel Montoya well. They had come up through the ranks together. Bernardo was shocked at the murder of his friend. Who would have the audacity to do such a thing? Miguel was a powerful politician in the APRA, one of President Garcia's strongest supporters and confidantes. This had to have been well planned and precisely executed. Men like Montoya were rarely unguarded, and the locals would never dare to try anything so foolish. Besides, he was popular with the people. And this list; he glanced at the scrap of paper. Who would know such things? He saw his own name, his first and second and third names scattered on the piece of paper—Bernardo, then Jorge, and in another area, Fuento. Golden Traitors? He shook his head, puzzled by the news. "I'll need time," he said to his friend.

"Time may be what we have very little of," the general replied. "I'll leave it in your hands. *We* will leave it in your hands," he corrected himself, and then rose from his chair.

Bernardo also stood, and then hesitated. "You said there were two things we needed to discuss. What was the second?"

Victor stiffened, and then stared directly into his friend's eyes with a look of both sadness and empathy. He sat down again and stared at the floor. "It's about Emelia," he said, still staring at the floor.

"What about Emelia?" Bernardo asked. What was the general going to say? He felt a knot tighten in his abdomen.

"The circumstances…." He hesitated.

"What? What *circumstances?*"

"Bernardo, my friend, this is difficult for me, please." He waved his hand as if to fan himself from the intensity of what he was about to say. "Emelia, she…when her body was autopsied, it was not considered entirely a *natural* death."

"What are you saying? Not a natural death? She lay dying in my arms in Ancón not more than a few days ago. She had a heart attack. The doctors…I saw them take her into the hospital with my own eyes! They said it was a heart attack. What are you getting at?" He felt his voice growing louder and higher. He was feeling light-headed. Victor continued to stare at the floor.

"What the hell, Victor? What are you saying? Tell me now!" he demanded.

"When the coroner performed a routine series of tests at the morgue, before they took the body for cremation, there were signs of curare poisoning, along with a slight neck wound, a pinprick, really; the kind a dart might make." Victor looked his friend straight in the eyes now.

"And you didn't see the need to tell me about these tests or the results until now?? Why not, Victor?" Bernardo was now inches away from his friend's face. His breathing was coming in ragged breaths. He was angry.

"It would have done little good for you at the time, my friend; you were already so upset. We began our own investigation before you went back to Ancón. I'm sorry to burden you with this, Bernardo, but I felt I had to tell you now." He stood and reached to put his big hands on Bernardo's shoulders, but Bernardo pulled back.

"What are you saying? What does this mean? Are you saying my wife was killed? She was poisoned?" He felt dizzy. The room began to spin. He thought he was going to faint. Perspiration began to drip off his forehead. He grabbed for a handkerchief from his pocket and wiped his brow, collapsing back into the chair.

"Bernardo, there are large forces at work here. It involves you, and me, and many of our friends, and possibly Emelia herself. I have no answers for you yet. We're investigating. I needed to bring you in on this for your help. I'm sorry this has brought you even more pain. I know how you loved your wife; we all did. I'll give you all the information I have in a few days. Please be patient." He stretched out his right hand to help Bernardo out of his chair. "Are you all right?"

"No, I'm not all right. Not at all." Bernardo decided to stop talking. It would do no good. His head was spinning. He needed to get out of the palace and clear his head to think.

He took the offered hand and rose slowly, putting his handkerchief back in his pocket. What the hell? He tried to focus on his friend but was having difficulty.

"Victor, I can't do this anymore tonight; I must go. Perhaps we can meet again tomorrow. I must…go to the apartment." He rose and headed absently towards the door, as if in a dream. He didn't feel his body at all. It was as if he was watching a scene unfold from a film. His mind was going numb from the information he had just been given.

Victor walked Bernardo towards the door. On his way out, Victor gave Bernardo a sympathetic look. "You cannot fail to find this person, or people, my friend. There is, as you know, much at stake. I'll call you in the morning." Bernardo softly closed the door behind him as he let himself out of the room.

Victor watched on the security camera as the car slipped away into the night. He walked down the cobblestone hallway and returned to his quarters, where he picked up the secure phone by his bed. He dialed a pre-set number on his phone.

"He's been briefed," he said quietly into the phone, almost at a whisper. "I think he's bought into the conspiracy plot. He's still grieving the loss of his wife. I had him at an advantage. He's weak right now. Poor bastard doesn't even have a clue what's going on." He sighed into the phone. There was silence on the other end of the line.

"Send some men, some nobodies, and take him out at his apartment in the morning. You know, the one in Miraflores? I need marksmen, not amateurs, comprende?"

"Si," was the only response he got from the entire conversation, and the line went dead.

He hung up the phone, sighed again, and began removing his uniform and boots. *Hopefully,* he thought to himself, *this last threat will be over by tomorrow morning.* Bernardo, his friend of many years, was too close to this situation. He'd known him for a long time. He knew he was way too smart to not figure out the pieces of the puzzle sooner or later. Victor was sad to lose him, and especially sad about not telling him about his wife. They were such good friends. But this was about business, and vast fortunes…not friendship. After he was dead, they could become friends again. Sort of. He chuckled to himself, and turned off the light.

CHAPTER THREE - EMELIA

1957

Emelia Mercedes Sanchez Podera was the oldest of three girls in her family. Her mother had prayed to bring her husband a boy for over 10 years. She would go every day, as good Catholics do, into La Catedral in the center of the city and light a candle and pray to St. Gerard, *"O glorious Saint Gerard, powerful intercessor before God, and wonder worker of our day, I call upon you and seek your help. You, who always fulfilled God's will on earth, help me to do God's holy will. Intercede with the Giver of life, from whom all parenthood proceeds, that I may conceive and raise a boy who will please God and my husband in this life, and be heir to the Kingdom of Heaven. Amen."* She and her husband certainly had tried, and prayed, but it seemed God wanted to favor the Podera family with beautiful girls: Emelia, Anna, and Violeta.

Jorge Podera, her father, was a successful merchant. He exported many different commodities from his offices in Lima and Cuzco, from grains, to merino wool, to minerals. Jorge was a native of Cuzco, born in the Urubamba Valley, the *Valle Sagrado* or Sacred Valley. It was here, long ago, that his Inca ancestors had lived and thrived for centuries, before the Spaniards came in the 1500s and decimated his people. His native Quechua tongue had served him well over the years when negotiating with the local wool traders. Their common hatred of the Spanish was only an additional bond in getting the best deal with the local herdsmen.

His wife, Maria, stayed home and took care of the girls. From time to time, towards the end of the summer, they would travel to the seaside village of Ancón and take holiday there for a month. It was a glorious little village full of life and sun, and most of all, the beaches. The girls practically lived on the sand and in the sea when they visited the resort village. Although the family preferred the mountains of Cuzco, and the beauty of the surrounding valleys and rivers, the beach had its own particular fascination.

One summer day, which started out as so many others, the girls had traipsed down to the beach with their *abuela*, Nana, who was a constant chaperone, keeping a sharp eye on the girls and any stray boys who might wander too close by. But Nana was getting on in years, and had a hard time keeping up with her energetic grandchildren. They would run endlessly up and down the beach with the kite she had helped them fashion, which only led to her quickly retiring to a comfortable chair and umbrella with a good vantage point.

A young boy who offered to help her fix the tail of her kite startled Emelia. He had brown eyes and was dark and tan from the sun, and his brown hair had slight hints of red from the sun and sea. She knew better than to show any interest at all, especially under the watchful eye of her grandmother, but something about the boy disarmed her. He was so helplessly awkward, and stammered through his words. What a silly boy. Her sisters were giggling at the exchange between them. He even ran down the beach to his own towel and ripped a piece off to fix the tail of her kite. But, there was something about him she found rather…she searched for the word in her mind. It was a feeling she had not experienced before, except perhaps in books. It was a type of excitement, energy—it was very unusual.

After he had tied the strip of towel to the tail, they ran together down the beach to watch the kite climb and swoop until it was high in the sky. As they stood and watched the kite, her sisters jumping up and down with excitement, he introduced himself as Bernardo. She told him her name, and quickly handed him the kite and thanked him as

"Señor Ingeniero," then ran away for home, leaving him there, trapped with the kite, unable to follow. Grandmother was asleep in her chair under the umbrella. The girls ran through the crowded boulevard and darted down a small alley towards their summer apartment. Anna and Violeta giggled and teased Emelia about "the boy" on the beach, and how she acted around him.

"You liked him, didn't you?" Anna laughed. Violeta was barely old enough to understand, except to seize any opportunity to give her sister a hard time. She was the youngest, and used to getting all the attention, especially from Papa whom they all adored.

"I'm telling Papia" she announced triumphantly, and stuck her tongue out at Emelia. Emelia feigned anger at her little sister, running after her.

"You'd better not, you little mouse, or I'll find a big cat to eat you up!" She chased after her, claws extended and hissing. The girls all screamed and ran up the stairs, laughing, and breathlessly pushed through the front door and collapsed in a heap on the rug in the front hallway. Their mother rushed down the stairs to see what all the commotion was about.

"What on earth are you silly girls making so much noise about? Your Papa is trying to take a nap."

"Oh, Mama," Violeta said, pushing her way out of the pile to be first to tell the news. "Emelia found her kite in sharming ardor!"

"What?" her mother said, starting to laugh. The other girls looked at each other and fell on the floor laughing. Violeta was puzzled, and then mad. She had delivered the information that would surely get her sister in trouble, yet they were laughing.

"What's so funny?" she demanded, turning a little red in the face; her plan was failing right in front of her eyes.

"That's a KNIGHT IN SHINING ARMOR!" Anna and Emelia said at the same time, and laughed again hysterically.

"But it *was* a kite!" Violeta said, confused.

Their mother interrupted their shrieking. "Girls, you need to go get a broom and clean up this sand you've spilled all over the floor," she said firmly, still smiling at her youngest. Little Violeta, always trying so hard to be a grown-up. She loved her probably the most, she thought to herself, as she scooted the children towards the closet where the broom and dustpan were kept. "And go outside and wash off all that sand! I don't want you tracking that all over our nice clean apartment!" She paused a moment, looking around. "Where is your nana?" She found it odd that her ever-vigilant mother was not on their heels.

"We left her asleep down on the beach, Mama," Emelia replied. Maria thought it best to go get her and bring her home for supper. The sun would be too harsh for the old woman at this time of day. So, she set out for the boardwalk.

"I'm going to get Nana, girls. You stay here and clean up!" She climbed down the stairs and headed for the beach.

Emelia thought about the boy, Bernardo, as she swept up the sand on the hallway floor. He was attractive, but very impolite. He was clever, that was clear. The way he had fixed her kite...her kite! Oh, Mama would be furious that she gave him her kite; but she was in such a rush to get away...why had she been in such a rush? Her mind whirred.

"Emelia!" She heard her name being called, but was too busy thinking about the boy. "Emelia! Look what you're doing!" her sister scolded, looking up at her from the floor. She was holding the dustpan, but Emelia was simply sweeping the sand without looking down. Was she sleepwalking?

"Emelia! Watch what you're doing. You're getting sand all over the place!" Anna grabbed the end of the broom and shook it. "Hey, up there in the clouds; you, Emelia!" Emelia suddenly broke her concentration and was startled.

"Oh!" she exclaimed. "I'm sorry, Anna. I don't know what I was thinking."

Anna looked up at her and used that whiney voice that Emelia hated. "Look, you've made an even bigger mess than before we started! Mama will be furious with us if we don't get this done." Emelia hurriedly swept the pile of sand together, and then neatly into the dustpan.

"I'm sorry, Anna. I don't know what I was doing," she said absently.

"You don't know how to sweep the floor anymore? Are you sick?" her sister asked, laughing. Emelia looked down at her sister and scowled.

"Just throw the sand outside and let's get this put away," she said, and walked towards the closet to put the broom back in its place.

***

Maria hurried down the lane towards the beach. It was a hot January afternoon, and she was annoyed with the girls for messing up the hallway, although it was a funny story about the boy and Emelia. She smiled to herself and thought of the boy on the beach, and remembered the first time she was *enamoro*. Her mind drifted back in time to the schoolyard in her hometown of Venturosa. *What was that boy's name?* she thought to herself, navigating across the boulevard and looking up and down the beach. Finally she spotted her mother, fast asleep in a chair, umbrella barely giving her any shade with the shift of the afternoon sun.

"Mama!" she called, as she hurried towards her. "Mama, you will get so sunburned out here!" She was puzzled as to why she didn't respond. Her mother had never slept well, and when she did, it was as if she were a cat, always hearing everything. Nothing escaped her ears, day or night. "Mama!" she repeated again loudly, as she scooped off her sandals and hurried through the hot sand to her chair.

She arrived, slightly out of breath, and shouted, "Mama! Why aren't you home?" She shook her shoulder to wake her. Her body simply moved to one side and then slumped onto the sand, headfirst. "Mama?" she cried, and ran around the chair, dropping to her knees and lifting under her shoulders. The old woman's head draped backwards towards her, upside down like a broken marionette, mouth open and eyes staring into nothingness. "Mama? Oh no, oh, Mama, no!" she began to sob, and pulled her mother's head to her chest. "No!" she screamed. People came running from all directions, but of course, it was too late.

Maria Podera was in mourning for months. Neither Papa nor other family members could console her. After they had returned grandmother's body to Lima, there was no peace in the Podera household for many, many months. The girls had been hurriedly packed up by their maids and put on the train back to Lima. They were not given any time to grieve, or even react to the loss of their beloved Nana. It had all happened so suddenly. Family members arrived from out of town and out of the country. The girls were told to be quiet, and were dressed in black mourning dresses. The funeral was a somber affair on a foggy day in late January. There were aunts and uncles and cousins, and people she had never even seen before, paying their respects to the family. Emelia had gone from the heights of her first glimpse of love to the depths of despair all in one day. It was a day she would never forget.

For a long time, Mama would just stay in her bedroom with the curtains drawn. From time to time, Emelia would hear her crying. Many times she had tried to console her mother, coming to her at all hours to hug her, only to be pushed away.

"Leave me alone, Emelia!" she would scream at her. Emelia would leave in tears. She had never lost anyone she loved. She didn't know the rules. Papa was either gone at work all day, or in the bedroom with Mama at night, for what seemed like months. The girls had to fend for themselves. Fortunately, they had each other, and cried and consoled one another. But children are resilient, and grieving does not last forever; after all, life was still all looking forward for them, not backwards.

Chapter Four - Bernardo

Present Day

Bernardo had not slept well. He arose early the next morning and looked out over the expanse of the Pacific Ocean from his apartment window. He was on the tenth floor of a fairly modern apartment building in Miraflores, not far from where he had grown up. The old house had been sold many years ago, after he and his brother and sister had grown up. Papa had died in 1973, but not before becoming partner of one of the largest conglomerate banks in Peru. Fortune had smiled on the Villacorta family, and as the years had passed, Papa had gotten more and more well known for his skills, first as a scrupulously detail-oriented accountant, then becoming a financial advisor for some of the wealthier families in Lima, and finally a successful banker. He died peacefully in his sleep. Mama died several years later of cancer. It had ravaged her body, and despite all the medical advice and care money could buy, all that the chemotherapy and radiation had done was to weaken her, and ultimately take her faster. She died in agony nearly three years to the day that she had been diagnosed.

The weather was typical of Lima in the late summer; balmy and humid. It usually took the better part of the morning before the sun burned off the fog that covered the ocean and the coast. By midafternoon, the surfers were lined up to catch the endless waves that rolled onto the shores of Lima, looking like tiny floating corks balanced on toothpicks bobbing up and down in the shiny waves. Bernardo sipped his morning tea and thought about the previous night's meeting. His wife had been killed? The thought sickened him. This changed everything, he thought, with his teeth clenched. The murders of his wife and his friend Montoya were both a warning and an announcement. Whoever it was, or whatever group was represented by the execution, knew much more than he could have ever imagined. He pulled the copy of the scrap of paper the general had given him last night out of his pocket and examined it. Typed. Some of the letters were only partially filled in with ink, especially the *o*'s, which was not that unusual for an old typewriter that had been used a lot. It was a vowel, and thus typed more often than other letters. As such it was worn down, flatter than the others. He noticed the same with the *e*'s and the *a*'s. Hard, if not impossible to trace, especially in the old-fashioned city of Lima, where typewriters were still found in many homes and offices. Curiously, the ñ did not seem as worn. And then, of course, there was the cotton thread with the knots, the quipu. This worried him the most.

He left the copy of the paper and the thread on the dining room table and walked to the Asiro original on his wall, and lifted it off of its hanger. On the bare wall was a safe, with a retinal scan biometric device. He walked to the device, putting his chin in the holder so that his face was just close enough for the right eye to be scanned. A green light lit up on the panel, and a slight noise of bolts being withdrawn into the wall followed. He pulled the door open and looked inside the small, well-lit safe. There were three shelves; one for his passports on the left, and stacks of various foreign currencies on the right. The second shelf held two Beretta Px4 Storm 9mm pistols, loaded, with four 17-round magazines neatly stacked next to the guns. The third shelf held one small item. A USB 512KB drive with a small lanyard for not losing it, he supposed. Of course losing it, or more importantly, its contents, would certainly cost him his life, and the lives of many others. He took the USB drive and shut the door to the safe. After carefully placing the painting back in its place, he walked over to his desk and turned on his laptop.

He placed the thumb drive into the USB port on the side of his laptop and selected an encrypted document from a long list of files. To the untrained eye, they looked like "garbage characters" ¤ό€ψΩÏД•ŧℓƎ ffⅠ№Ω. But upon clicking on the file, he was prompted for a password key, and after entering it, the file opened with an "access granted" message. He kept all the files he owned highly encrypted. At 512-bit encryption, it would be virtually impossible to crack these files without the key. Just another safety measure to assure that in the event of a disaster, these files would be secure.

The file opened to reveal a detailed list of GPS latitudes and longitudes, along with names, addresses, phone numbers, bank accounts, and links to personal financial statements in yet another file. Something nagged at him that had escaped his attention initially, but he went back to it now. Under the main directory details, he scanned the dates modified. Several of the files had dates going back to 2004. Three of the files had dates that had been changed three days ago, including the one he was looking at. He had not personally opened any of these files for at least three months, yet they clearly had been opened, examined, and no doubt, copied. He felt a tightening in his gut as his mind began to race with the sinking feeling that his entire security system had been compromised. But how, and by whom?

He closed the file, pulled out the thumb drive, and returned it to the safe, then replaced the painting on the wall once again. Shutting off his laptop, he sipped on some fresh Mate de Coca tea to clear his mind, and began to analyze what he had just discovered. Whatever the reason for the compromise, it had already cost the life of a friend, and perhaps his own wife. If what he feared was actually the case—that the files themselves had been hacked—there was serious cause for alarm. Many lives and vast fortunes were involved. Whoever it was clearly had unlimited resources at his or her disposal to gain access to this information. No one had access to his apartment but the building manager and Bernardo's housekeeper, a woman he had known for fourteen years. In all that time, she had quietly come and gone, cleaning and washing with thorough efficiency. Johanna had been faithfully prompt and dedicated to her job for all these years. He paid her very well. He and Emelia knew her children. He found it hard to believe that she would betray him.

Antonio, the building supervisor, had been with the building since he had moved in over 15 years ago. He was very security conscious, constantly watching all the monitors that surrounded the building. His counterpart for the evening shift, Hernando, was younger, and had been there only about a year. Still, there was nothing Bernardo ever did or said by the way he came and went that would arouse suspicion, or give away who he really was. As far as the staff was concerned, he was a kindly, middle-class businessman who wore modest clothing, drove a modest used car, and drew very little attention to himself. Of course, there had been visitors over the years, but no one of any interest. He was often gone on "business trips" for months at a time. As far as the building supervisor and owners were concerned, the rent was always paid in advance, and he was never late.

He returned to his list of people as possible suspects. Hernando was the logical choice. The phone rang. "Hello?" he said.

A familiar voice spoke to him on the line. "I was hoping you were back in town! Are you available for lunch today?" His friend Arturo, whom he had known since university, was a welcome voice to hear.

"Arturo! How are you, my friend? Of course; where and when?"

"What about El Pez Amigo, say around two this afternoon?" Bernardo knew the restaurant well. It was one of his favorites; only open for a few short hours each day to guarantee the fish was fresh and the food, perfect. They did a thriving business with the locals, and had been in the same location for over twenty years.

"Great. I'll see you at two, my friend. Ciao," he said, and hung up.

Bernardo reached to pick up his teacup from the table when the window behind him suddenly exploded into thousands of tiny pieces. Instinctively, he hit the floor and rolled in the direction of the nearest wall that would shield him from the direction of what he suspected was a shot. There was no sound other than the usual street noise below. *Silencer,* he thought to himself, as he cautiously peeked around the corner of the wall just to catch a quick look in the direction of the shot. A few shards of tempered glass were still hanging in the seal around the frame. He estimated the shot had come from a building approximately 100 meters away. He glanced back at the wall. There was a bullet embedded about a meter up from the floor, indicating the shot had to have come from a higher elevation than he was. He ducked out again and back. A loud whistle passed close to his protected space and popped into the wall fairly close to the last one. Still there, *mierda!* This was insane! He was being fired upon in his own apartment! One last quick look, and then he had to move. He ducked the right side of his head out again, scanned the building, and ducked back to the protection of the wall. He'd spotted a figure with a rifle on top of the building. The sniper had a scope and a tripod. This guy was not an amateur. He rolled away from the wall backwards. Another whistle, and a bullet slammed through the wall he had been hiding behind and blasted into a dining room chair, shattering the wood into toothpicks. He fumbled for the cell phone in his pocket and dialed Señor Isidro, his friend in the Serenazgo of Miraflores. "Allo?" said the voice on the other end.

"Matteo, it's me, Bernardo," he said, panting slightly from the adrenaline rush.

"Oh, Señor Villacorta! What can I do for you, señor?" he said in a happy, almost too-cheerful voice.

"Matteo, please, I need your help NOW! Someone is shooting at my apartment, and they are quite good. I'm afraid they will kill me if I don't get some help soon!" he said with all the urgency he could muster.

"What? Where are you, señor?"

"I'm in my apartment, on Malecón Cisneros. The shots are coming from the northwest on a building on Roma. Hurry, please!"

"We'll be there in two minutes, señor!" he assured, his voice suddenly all business. The line went dead. Bernardo waited. About thirty seconds later he heard sirens approaching in the distance. He looked at his watch. He let three minutes go by, and slid back over to his previous vantage point. He again snuck a quick view around the corner and through the shattered window. There were many men with weapons, dressed in uniforms, scattered about the roof. His cell phone rang.

"Señor Villacorta? We have secured the roof. There is evidence of a shooter, but no one is here now. Whoever it was has gone. I have shell casings and we're scouring the building. I also have called the police. This is a matter for them. May I have them come speak with you?"

"Of course," Bernardo answered. "Can you have them bring those shell casings, too?"

"Si." The phone fell silent again.

Feeling relatively sure he was not going to be fired upon, Bernardo got off the floor and walked around the broken glass to the kitchen to get a broom. He found himself sweating and shaking. This was not the best way to start the day. Soon there was a beep on his apartment phone. He lifted it and asked who it was, although he already knew.

"Señor Villacorta, this is Captain Andreas Sanchez of the Lima Police. May I come up to speak with you please?"

"Certainly," he answered, and buzzed him in. The elevator arrived, and three officers came in, one immediately going to the shattered windows and signaling another on the roof of the building he had suspected the shots came from.

The captain stepped forward and extended his hand. "I'm Captain Sanchez, señor, and you must be Señor Villacorta." He smiled politely.

"Yes, that's me," Bernardo said.

"You have had an exciting morning," remarked the captain. "May I sit down, señor?"

"Please," said Bernardo, and gestured towards the sofa. He sat down to his right in a large armchair.

"Do you object if my men take a look around and do some tests?"

"No, of course not," Bernardo replied. "I was hoping you could tell me what the hell is going on," he muttered in an off-handed fashion.

"I was hoping you might tell me the same thing, señor. It would seem someone doesn't like you very much. Any idea who that could be?" The captain pulled two shell casings from his jacket pocket (*great police work,* Bernardo thought, *now everyone's fingerprints are on them*) and placed them on the glass coffee table between them. "I make them to be .300 caliber Winchester Magnum; shell casing is from Black Hills. Standard issue for most sniper rifles."

Bernardo picked up one of the casings with the end of a pen, to emphasize his point about police stupidity, and examined it. The captain knew his ammunition. "I have no enemies that I know of," Bernardo lied. "I'm just a Lima-based importer," he said, again lying, but looking as sincere and frightened as he could. The captain's men were lining up lasers from the building to the holes in his walls. They scribbled down notes and took pictures with small digital cameras. Bernardo placed the casing back on the table next to the other one.

"Señor Villacorta, have there ever been any attempts on your life before? Do you know anyone that might want to hurt you or your family?" he asked.

"I have no family, Captain. In fact, I just returned last night from burying my wife in Ancón."

"Oh, I see. I'm sorry for your loss," he said, as sincerely as possible. It was clear the captain was not satisfied with the answers to his questions. He knew, as any seasoned police officer would, that people who don't have enemies, don't typically have other people shooting at them with sniper rifles from well-planned vantage points. Nor do the shooters evade police easily and leave nothing behind but what they want to have discovered. The shell casings were a calling card of sorts. Also a warning. The captain was assuming that if the sniper had wanted to, he could have taken out Villacorta on the first shot, and probably had ample time to set up the shot as well. No, something was not right here. "Perhaps you could tell me where you have been over the past couple of days, Señor Villacorta, besides Ancón." He leaned forward, expecting an answer, while he studied Bernardo's face.

Bernardo had decided it was time to end this conversation; he had things to do. "Captain, I'll give my friend General de la Hoya a call; perhaps he can assist you," Bernardo replied, and reached for his cell phone.

"General *Victor* de la Hoya, señor?" the captain practically gasped. "No, ah, no, I don't think that will be necessary, señor. I'm sure we can conduct this investigation without disturbing you any longer." And finishing his sentence, he barked orders at the two other men, who immediately stopped what they were doing, packed up their equipment, and stepped quickly into the elevator. The captain rose from the couch, bowed slightly, and said, "I'm sure we may need to contact you at some future time, Señor Villacorta. I hope this has not been an inconvenience for you. I'll have my men stationed around the area for a few days to assure this does not happen again. Good day, sir." He walked stiffly to the elevator, the door closed, and the elevator descended.

The captain cursed quietly to himself. *No enemies my ass!* he thought to himself. The very fact that General de la Hoya was a friend of his said it all. This was way too big for him. He would call the National Police to handle the remainder of the investigation. The policemen rode to ground floor in total silence.

Bernardo returned to the safe again, opened it, and reached for one of the Beretta Px4 Storm 9mm pistols. He took another clip, stuffing them into his pocket. He shut the safe and sat down on the couch. The Beretta dug into his side. He made a mental note to get his holster, and removed the gun from his pocket. Cradling it in his hands, he remembered long ago when he'd purchased his first gun.

His first firearm purchase was not as simple as the ones he had "given" to him nowadays. When he was younger, as business improved, he began to transport large sums of money to and from the bank. Everything was paid in cash, especially payroll, so Bernardo began to feel the need to be armed when he came from the bank. Even though it was a short distance to the office, he was always vulnerable.

No one trusted anyone in Peru. A simple bank transaction was an opportunity to be robbed through a vigilant telephone call from the bank teller to a friend, giving Bernardo's description and the sum of money he was carrying. He would be followed by several unassuming men, and when the time was opportune, jumped, and relieved of his money. Often, the determining factor to foil the theft was simply a gun. Guns were unusual weapons in Peru and very hard to get, even for criminals. He had bought his first *pistola* in a gun shop, and was then told he would receive it after he got his permit. He was handed three originals of sale; a written bill of sale, a certificate from the gun shop with their authorization, and a list of instructions and forms to follow. Once completed, he was to return to the store, and his gun would be waiting for him.

"If you're very persistent, it will take about two weeks," the gun shop owner told him. *Persistent* was a code word for bribery. The more people you bribed, the faster the process went.

First, a trip to the Ministry of the Interior, where, after showing his papers and a 50-sole note, he was shown to another location where he would receive his "mental exam."

He filled out the necessary forms, and paid the bank fees (and a little more). Then he was immediately ushered past a room full of waiting men, and into a small room where he was given a written test of about forty questions. The test took about half an hour, and then was graded by a psychologist. He was asked a series of verbal questions; Did he drink? Did he smoke? Was he ever involved in physical altercations with his friends? Did he feel depressed? And so on, for another half-hour. At the end he was pronounced fit, and given a shiny certificate proclaiming same, and for 10 soles, he was on to the next process. Back to the Ministry of the Interior, this time to be cleared for no prison record, no arrest record, and no police record (but that would have to be done at the National Police Headquarters office in Miraflores). Unfortunately, on that particular day, the "system was down," which he wasn't told until standing in the heat of summer for about two hours. He took a cab to another office in Miraflores. They insisted on a color picture. There just so happened to be such a person right at the gate. He led Bernardo off to his "studio," which doubled as a *cevichera*, and took his picture.

"It will be ready in two days, señor," he was told, and was given a receipt. Two days later, picture and papers in hand, he went back to the Ministry of the Interior, got his papers stamped, and was sent to the National Police. Once cleared there, he was sent back to the Ministry of the Interior to get his final papers stamped and certified by at least three more officials. Word would be sent to him when he could go back to the store and receive his gun.

The Ministry of Defense kept all guns in a centralized repository. The serial number of the gun was assigned to Bernardo, and only Bernardo. And then, with yet another permit approved by a few more officials, it was transported to the gun store. This was life in Peru. It took three weeks before he was holding his Brazilian Taurus .357 Magnum for the first time. From that moment on, the gun never left his side. He only had to show it once, to a man who quite accidently bumped into him as he left the bank with about $20,000 in his briefcase. Bernardo pushed him back and opened his coat to display the gun, his hand already on the handle. The man jumped back instinctively, insisting his innocence and pleading for forgiveness. It would have been hard to say who was more frightened.

CHAPTER FIVE

Bernardo was still shaking slightly as he descended in the elevator to the basement of his apartment building to get his car and drive to lunch. He walked to the 2004 Honda Accord and stopped for a moment. He had come home in a cab the night before. The car had not been used for over two weeks. He twirled the set of keys in his hand and looked around. There was no one else in the garage. He got down on his knees on the right side of the car and peered carefully underneath, scanning from the front to the rear for any unusual shapes. In view of what had just happened, it wouldn't be that remarkable to have an "insurance package" waiting for him in case the sniper missed. He pulled a small device from his jacket pocket, extended a flexible wand from the end and waved it under, over, and around the Honda. The light remained green, indicating no obvious evidence of C4, Semtex, dynamite, or liquid explosives.

Bernardo opened the door, got in, and held his breath while he turned the key. The engine started up. He breathed a little sigh of relief. He pulled out of the garage and headed towards the restaurant. As he drove, his mind was racing, making checklists of things that needed to be investigated, and people he needed to get in touch with. With the National Police already involved, it would be hard to keep this quiet for very long. He noticed the reporters out in front of the building as he turned to the right and proceeded down the winding road that hugged the coastline. Instinctively, he scanned his rearview mirror to watch for tails. Nothing out of the ordinary caught his scan of the road behind him. He turned off on a side street to backtrack towards his destination of the restaurant. As he made yet another turn, he noticed a black motorcycle pull in behind him and stay at a discreet distance from the rear of his vehicle, never too close, but never falling very far behind. Bernardo gunned the Honda and cut into traffic, watching in his rearview mirror. The motorcycle sped up, deftly maneuvered between cars, and quickly fell in place behind him again. He was being followed. The question now was for what purpose; to see where he was going, or something more malevolent?

Bernardo saw an open space on the side of the road and quickly slid into the space without signaling, then came to a complete stop. The motorcycle did not have time to react, and had to keep on going or give himself away. Bernardo pulled out almost immediately and sped up behind the motorcycle. The driver had to be a man, with such broad shoulders. He was dressed in typical black leathers, with a dark helmet concealing any features of the head. The hunter had become the hunted, at least for a moment. Without notice, the motorcycle accelerated quickly and sped away, weaving in and out of traffic, and finally out of sight.

Quite a morning, Bernardo mused to himself. He doubled back again, went at least two miles out of his way, and then doubled back *again* to the restaurant. He saw no one else follow him. Emilio, the security guard in front of El Pez Amigo, waved and motioned him into a spot directly in front of the door to the restaurant.

Emilio hurried over and opened the door. "Buenos tardes, señor." Bernardo smiled at the security guard. Emilio had started years ago as just a local kid, hustling to clean cars while patrons dined. Over the years he had gone into the military, and after finishing his four years, joined the Serenazgo for a while. Then he found the private security sector more lucrative. He had been at El Pez Amigo for almost 12 years now. "Shall I give your car a little cleaning while you eat, señor?" Old habits die hard.

"Of course; thank you, Emilio," Bernardo acquiesced, and threw him the keys. He walked into the restaurant and scanned the small room for his friend, Arturo. He was sitting by the window in their familiar spot, two glasses of sparkling water waiting, and a large helping of fresh ceviche between the two places.

"Ah, my friend, mucho gusto!" said Arturo, and he rose and gave Bernardo a hug and a kiss on the cheek. They hugged again and sat down.

"So," Arturo said first. "So much tragedy since last we spoke. I'm so sorry about Emelia, my friend; you know that, of course. There are no words that would be adequate, so I'll speak no more about this, but to say I am heartbroken for you."

"Thank you, amigo," Bernardo said, as he looked down at his plate. With all the insanity that had occurred in the past day, he had almost forgotten. "Ceviche?" He motioned to the large, colorful plate filled with tiny pieces of fresh fish, hot peppers, and onions, with slabs of sweet potatoes surrounding the raw fish concoction.

"Of course." Arturo filled his small plate with the uniquely Peruvian delicacy. The fish was raw, but "cooked" in spiced lime juice so that it literally melted in one's mouth. It was a specialty of the house, and never disappointed. They both ate quietly for a minute or two, savoring the flavors of the ceviche.

"How are Camilla and the kids?" Bernardo asked. The "kids" were now full-grown adults, but they had known each other for so long, they were still children in his mind. And he was, after all, their godfather.

"Camilla is fine. She's had some problems with her 'plumbing,' and you know that begins to happen at her age...but other than that, she's fine. Fernando has gotten a job with Minera Majaz, a mining company down in the Amazon area. He's been a bit concerned about some of their practices. It's rumored that they are exploiting the locals down there and when they protest in any way, things...happen...you know what I mean? So, he's looking for another position with another company. He's making very good money there, but is not very comfortable with management's practices, I guess you might say."

"And Elena? Has she finished her studies for becoming a surgeon?"

"Yes," said Arturo, his pride showing slightly on his face. "She's one of the first female otolaryngologists to be picked by the government to conduct reconstructive surgery on children in the Andes regions. She's very happy, and of course, we're so proud of the work she's doing for our people who cannot afford this kind of care." Bernardo nodded approvingly. Emelia would have been so proud of this news.

As Arturo was talking, he'd reached into his inside jacket pocket and pulled out an ordinary envelope, which was quite full. He laid it on the table in front of Bernardo. Scribbled on the front were three words: *por su ayuda* (for your help).

"What's that?" Bernardo inquired.

"I don't know," said his friend. "I thought you might help me figure it out."

"What would I know of this?" Bernardo examined the envelope without touching it.

"Because it has your name on a list of names inside, along with almost 750,000 soles, that's why."

Bernardo was stunned. "May I see the list?"

"Of course." Arturo opened the fat envelope and extracted a handwritten list of names, handing it to his friend. It had an uncanny resemblance to the list he had seen from the previous night. Bernardo scanned the list, and at first started to hand it back to his friend, then stopped and put it in his pocket.

"If you don't mind, I'll keep this. Do you know any of these people besides me?" he asked.

"No, no one. That's why I had to see you. I thought you might be able to shed a little light on this. I don't like the looks of this, and this money. My God, I've never seen so much money in my life. What am I supposed to do?"

"Unfortunately, my friend, I think you've already done it. If anyone is watching us, which they no doubt are, you've confirmed my identity and threatened your own. I can't tell you much more except to say to literally, take the money and run. Gather up your wife and notify your children to hide. Leave the country, Arturo—tonight!"

"You must be joking, Bernardo." But he knew only too well by the grim look on his friend's face that he was deadly serious. They had suddenly both lost their appetites.

"Please. Put that envelope back in your pocket. I'm going to get up and go to the bathroom. After I have gone, please leave, and get Camilla and make arrangements to take a flight to somewhere far away for a while. I'll speak with you later."

Bernardo got up and smiled at Arturo, shook his hand, and stiffly walked towards the rear of the room to the bathrooms. Out of the corner of his eye, he saw Arturo rise and move towards the door. Bernardo passed the waiter and said, "La cuenta, por favor," and motioned to his table while he went into the bathroom. He felt a tightness in his gut. He had been identified, and was now surely a target himself, as if there hadn't been enough proof from this morning. He flipped open his cell phone and called the general.

"Yes?" a voice on the other end said.

"We have a problem, amigo. I need your help. I'm afraid I'm next on the list."

"Yes, I already heard about the incident this morning from the police. Why haven't you called me before now?"

"I was having lunch with a friend. He showed me a list like the one we found last night. He was also paid over 750,000 soles to show me the list in a public restaurant. I don't even think he knew what he was doing."

"Mierda!" muttered the general. "Where are you now?" he asked.

"El Pez Amigo in Miraflores; do you know it?"

"Of course. Sit tight. I'll send some of my men over to get you. They can be there in ten minutes. Can you find a way to stay there until then?"

"Yes, I think so," said Bernardo.

"All right. I'll have you brought here, and we'll figure how to proceed once you're safe. Be careful, my friend." Then he hung up.

Bernardo went through the motions of flushing the toilet and washing his hands, and returned to his table. The waiter was patiently waiting for him.

"Can I get you anything else, señor?" he asked.

"No, just the check, thank you."

The waiter pulled out a wireless device, punched a few keys and asked the usual question of all businessmen, "*Factura?*"

"No, not today, thank you." All business lunches or meals went through an elaborate process of paperwork, like everything in Peru, which included the company name, RUC number, address, and so on. And of course, the government got a piece of the action. Today it was way too much trouble, and he had a few other matters on his mind—like getting out of his favorite restaurant alive. He thought about his advice to Arturo. Probably wouldn't be a bad idea to do the same. While he waited, he thought of the possible places he could go to in the country that would be safe, or at least safer than Lima. He decided on Cuzco. He had a place in the Valle Sagrado that was not known by many people other than the locals. He would arrange for a private flight out this evening, and work on the details from the protection of the Andes. He flipped open his phone and hit autodial while he scanned the street for unusual activity as he spoke with his pilot.

"Geraldo. Fuel up the plane for a flight this evening around 20:00 hours to Cuzco. Please file the flight plans at the last moment, and be discreet about this. I'll meet you at the airport at 19:45. Be ready, and talk with no one about where you're going, or when. Do you understand?"

The voice at the other end of the phone said "Si, señor," and hung up.

A small armored vehicle pulled up suddenly in front of the restaurant. Two soldiers jumped out and entered the restaurant. Bernardo got up, and they motioned for him to follow. He caught the glance of Emilio as he left the restaurant.

"I'll be back for the car in a little while. Keep an eye on things till I return, yes?"

"Si," said Emilio, with a quizzical look at the army vehicle. Bernardo ducked inside, and the Iveco MPV rolled down the street towards the main artery into downtown. A radio crackled from the headset of the driver. He looked towards Bernardo and then back towards the road and muttered a response, no doubt letting his commander know that the "package" was safe and sound. The armored vehicle lumbered towards downtown at a crisp 30 kph.

Once they were close to the central area of Lima, the soldier on the passenger side flipped on lights and sirens and as if by magic, the massive traffic in front of them parted like the Red Sea once again. The vehicle weaved in and out of the narrow streets, and finally arrived at the same entrance at the rear of the Presidential Palace as the night before. Gates parted, papers were given and inspected, and the MPV descended into the lower levels of the palace.

Bernardo was escorted out of the vehicle and through the large wooden doors of the entrance. This time, his friend, General Victor de la Hoya, was waiting at the entrance to the hall.

Bernardo looked at him with a weak smile and said, "Thank you, my friend. It's been quite a day so far."

"Indeed," said the general, and put his large arm around his friend's shoulder, ushering him into another room. Two sentries snapped to attention as they entered. Victor waved them out of the room. The door was shut quietly, and they seated themselves in the overstuffed leather furniture once again.

"I have made some inquiries while I was waiting for your arrival," said the general. "It seems that the shooter from this morning was spotted on the roof by a few of the locals. We have a generalized description of him; approximately five foot four, dark hair in a ponytail of some sort, plaid shirt, jeans, and dark shoes. He fits about two or three hundred *thousand* possible suspects. We're looking. As far as your friend Arturo and the list and money, that is still a question mark. Do you have the copy of the list he gave you?"

"Yes," said Bernardo. He fished the piece of paper out of his shirt pocket and handed it to his friend. "The typing looks the same as the one you showed me last night. It looks similar."

"I, too, have something else to show you that might be of interest to you," said the general. "I know it got my attention this morning." He slid a piece of paper over to Bernardo, who picked it up and examined it. It was a bank statement from the Banco de Crédito de Perú with the general's name and home address on it. There had been a sizeable withdrawal several days before of over 750,000 soles. The bank statement was really an e-mail alert, notifying their renowned customer that a large amount of money had been withdrawn.

"So you see, I now know where that money came from for your friend. The only obvious question is, how was it done, and by whom? We're going over the videotapes of several branch offices for possible suspects. This could not have been done at an ATM. Someone who had very impressive credentials pulled this off, probably posing as me. I'll have to ask your friend for that money back, Bernardo; you know that." Bernardo nodded his head in agreement. He could cover the loss himself if necessary. It would be difficult to get the general to understand that he'd told his friend to take the money and run. "Do you have any reason to think that this friend of yours, Arturo, is involved in this in any way? He could be playing you."

"I cannot believe that," Bernardo said defensively. "I've known him for almost forty years. We've always been very close. It just doesn't make sense that he would sell me out like this. Besides, he has no idea about the cartel."

"So, he has just gone along with your cover story all this time? That you have risen up in the ranks of being a wealthy exporter, eh?"

"Yes, I'm sure of it." But it planted a seed of doubt in his mind. Was it possible? Had Arturo been approached? No one in Lima trusted anyone. It was a way of life. Plans, especially financial ones, were made, and remade and changed again just before execution to avoid any "complications," meaning robbery or kidnapping, or both.

He looked Victor in the eyes. "I'm going to disappear for a few weeks for protection, and to do some more investigating from a vantage point that is much safer than Lima. I'm leaving tonight."

"So, you're going to the old place in the Valle Sagrado, yes?"

It annoyed Bernardo that Victor guessed it so easily. But of course, if he couldn't trust the general, then all was lost.

"Perhaps," he said with a smile. "Victor, I'll have the money returned tonight. Do you want me to have it left with you?"

"That won't be necessary; I'm busy with other matters this evening. Just have our usual courier take care of it. I may have to bring your friend in for questioning, Bernardo. This concerns me a great deal."

"Please, Victor, let me handle this. I can get more information from him than you can. If we act too heavy-handed on this, it will arouse unnecessary suspicion, don't you think?"

"Perhaps," said the general. "All right, I'll give you forty-eight hours to get me something that makes me breathe a little easier, or we'll deal with things my way, understood?"

"Thank you, my friend," said Bernardo. "Can I get a lift back to pick up my car?"

"I've already arranged for your car to be returned to the garage at your apartment. One of my men will escort you home and wait for you until you're ready to go tonight." Bernardo smiled at his friend, and rose to give him a hug.

"Thanks, Victor. As always, you are on top of the details. I'll make contact with you in a day or so, once I get settled."

"Very well, amigo," said the general. "Just don't forget about your friend, Arturo...and the money!" He smiled, slapped his friend hard on the back, and led him out into the corridor to a waiting soldier. "And you are...?" he asked, leveling his gaze at the young soldier.

"Lieutenant Vasquez, sir!" he said, and snapped to attention.

"This is my very good friend, Señor Villacorta. You will take him wherever he wants, whenever he wants, and protect him with your life; is that understood?"

"Yes, sir!" came the reply, with another stiff boot snap.

"Good-bye, my friend," said Bernardo, "and thanks again for your help today."

"De nada," was the reply, as he saw the rather large rear end of his friend disappearing down the hallway, arm waving backwards towards him in a lazy manner. Bernardo jumped into the Mercedes, with the soldier at the wheel, and directed him to his apartment in Miraflores. There were a few items he needed to pick up before leaving. He looked at his watch. It was already nearing 6:00 p.m. and was dark outside. They had to hurry.

General Victor de la Hoya was cursing under his breath the entire length of the hall. What kind of screw-ups was he depending on for such an important task? How long could he keep up this ridiculous charade without tipping his hand in some way? If he moved on Bernardo again before he left Lima, it might cause even further suspicion. And between Arturo blowing his cover, and now that stupid captain of the

National Police was involved.… He saw a rat skitter down the hallway in front of him. He removed the Glock .45 from his side holster and shot with very precise aim at the rodent. It exploded all over the hallway and walls with a resounding blast that practically blew out his eardrums. Soldiers came running immediately, weapons drawn.

"It's all right. It's all right. Stand down!" he shouted through the smoke. "Just a damned rat!" The general's blood was boiling. "Get back to your damned posts!" he shouted at the men. He flipped open his cell phone and dialed a number. When the voice answered, he practically screamed into the cell phone, "Arturo, are you some kind of fool? All I asked you to do was to get your *friend* (he said through clenched teeth) into an open area where we could take the shot. You have failed me. I don't like failure, Arturo."

"But, but…." came the stammered reply from the other end of the line. "Please, General, give me one more opportunity," he pleaded. "I'm sure I can make this happen for you. It's just that I was so nervous. I'm a businessman, not an accomplice to murder!"

The general's tone settled into a quiet cadence. "No, that won't be necessary, Arturo. What will be necessary is that you, your wife, and your two children will have to pay for your unfortunate miscalculation."

"Oh no, General, please, not my family. Please, take me. You know where I am. Please, plea—"

"I know where all of you are," the general said in a low growl. "Good day, Arturo," and he flipped the phone shut. He opened it again, pressed another speed-dial number and said three words, "Do it now," and hung up again.

With those three words, two of his best snipers were dispatched to eliminate targets they had never met, but had been briefed on, in the event it was necessary.

CHAPTER SIX

Upon arriving at his apartment, Bernardo noticed that the shot-out window had already been neatly replaced and the glass cleaned up. It was as if nothing had ever happened. He gathered some clothes into a small bag, went to his safe, retrieved his Peruvian passport, 100,000 soles, the other Beretta and two extra clips, and the thumb drive. He threw them into his briefcase with his laptop, turned off the lights, and headed downstairs. The lieutenant was still waiting. Bernardo jumped into the back seat.

"Jorge Chavez, and step on it!" The soldier nodded and sped away. When they got close, Bernardo directed the driver to a smaller set of hangars to the south of the main airport off Elmer Faucett, the main road in front of the airport. Bernardo re-directed the driver to a private gate with armed security guards. The guards motioned the car to stop. They looked inside with flashlights, recognized Bernardo, and immediately motioned the guard tower to open the gates. The car continued towards a small hangar.

"You can stop here," said Bernardo, and got out of the car. He walked around to the driver's side and handed him a 100-sole note. "Thank you for your service, Lieutenant," he said, and walked towards the hangar. Inside was a sleek Gulfstream G150 that comfortably seated six. Geraldo, his pilot, was waiting outside the aircraft, which was already running. It was 19:45 exactly. Bernardo put a high price on promptness and efficiency, well known by anyone who worked for or with him. Geraldo was no exception.

"Our flight plan has been filed, señor, and we are wheels-up whenever you're ready, sir," said Geraldo, as he motioned for a young man nearby to take Bernardo's bag.

"That's fine," said Bernardo, and pulled the bag towards him. "I'll manage this, thank you." The young man backed off immediately. Bernardo climbed up the narrow stairs into the aircraft, the pilot close behind him. He threw his bag onto one of the leather seats towards the back, noting that several different newspapers were placed on the table next to his seat, along with fresh drinks, fruit, and various cheeses and meats. These items were all ingeniously fitted into small clear Plexiglas containers to prevent them from slipping during takeoff or turbulence.

The pilot pulled the cabin door shut and seated himself in the pilot's chair. The co-pilot was already seated and talking to the tower on the radio. "We'll be en route in about six minutes, señor," said the pilot. "We should arrive in Cuzco in a little over 55 minutes, at approximately 21:00 hours."

"Very well," said Bernardo. He kicked off his shoes, fastened his seat belt, and leaned back in his chair. He loved flying. The "group" had offered this slightly used jet as a reward for his faithful service over the years. Of course, it wasn't brand-new, but it really didn't matter to him. It almost seemed obscene that he was flying only himself to his home, when the plane could be used for so many more.

The jet taxied smoothly out of the hangar and down several side taxiways until it was queued up for takeoff. Within a few moments, he heard the chatter of the tower granting clearance. The pilot pushed the thrusters forward, and they rocketed down the main runway and up into the air. As they banked to the west, Bernardo gazed down at the glittering lights of Lima, and thought about the day's events. Once he got settled into the hacienda, he would have to put in some serious hours and detective work. There were too many loose ends, and he didn't like it. Besides, at this particular moment, he had not one clue that was helping him. He drifted off to sleep behind the white noise lull of the engines that had been throttled back to cruising speed.

He awoke just before landing in Cuzco, with the pilot announcing they were within 30 kilometers of the airport. Landing in Cuzco was tricky in the daytime, let alone at night. Cuzco Airport lay in a small patch in the Urubamba Valley, surrounded by the Andes Mountains. Navigating in was a test of any good pilot, starting with the 3,900-plus meters in altitude, not to mention the hard bank to the left and quick drop into the one and only runway. Geraldo had made this run so many times he could do it with his eyes closed, but Bernardo always watched closely, just in case.

Right on cue, the plane banked hard to the left, dropped altitude, and straightened out for its final approach. He could see the blue lights of the airstrip perfectly lined up with the nose of the jet. Geraldo touched down with barely a bump, flared the nose, and braked slowly, while turning off to a taxiway that took them to another small hangar on the west side of the airport. There was a black Mercedes waiting for them. Bernardo grabbed his bag, slipped on his shoes, and thanked Geraldo and Eduardo for the great flight. As he reached the hatch, he slipped the crew each an envelope of cash, 3,000 soles for the pilot, and 1,500 for the co-pilot.

They said, "Gracias, patron," and he descended the narrow stairs to the waiting car. He noticed the altitude immediately. To the inexperienced, Cuzco was a surprise. Breathing became difficult, and the lightheadedness that comes from the thin altitude of 3,395 meters was a potential problem unless you were used to it. The locals offered both coca tea and the bitter leaves to chew on until acclimation occurred. It usually took about twenty-four hours and some slight headaches. Water bottles were also essential; since one breathed harder and faster, the body released more water vapor and thus, dehydration was also a common issue for the tourists.

Many years ago, he'd had the vehicle fitted with an oxygen tank that would slowly filter pure oxygen into the car to ease the re-entry to this altitude. His driver offered to take his bag, which Bernardo declined, and he opened the rear door for Bernardo to get in. There was water and assorted drinks in the fold-out bar as well as fruit, cheeses, bread, and meat on a tray. It was cold in the mountains, and he shivered slightly as he climbed inside and grabbed a bottle of water, uncapped it, and drained it in a few long gulps. He grabbed a small pinch of dried coca leaves and popped them into his mouth, chewing them into a mushy paste that he left in the corner of his mouth. He had never liked the bitter juice, but it helped.

The car departed through the gates of the airport and headed northeast towards his hacienda in Yucay. His driver, Juan, had been with his family for over two generations. He was totally trustworthy, and rarely spoke.

"All is in order, and the staff are awaiting your arrival, señor," he said quietly as he drove towards *Nido de Búho* (the Owl's Nest), which Bernardo had always thought a fitting name for his hacienda; it was a place of both hiding, and observation of prey. He closed his eyes and slept fitfully as the car swept down the road towards the Valle Sagrado. They arrived close to midnight, and although the house was well-lit, the stars in the clear sky above were dazzling to him as he got out of the car and stretched. He thanked Juan, and told him he would see him in the morning. He opened the front door to the hacienda to be greeted by the four women who cared for the place; Alicia, Alejandra, Maria, and Melanie.

The two older women, Alicia the cook, and Maria, the chief housekeeper, warmly greeted their patron. *"Buenas noches, patron,"* they said with a slight bow.

"Buenas noches, señoras," he greeted back. The two younger girls, Alejandra and Melanie, remained still and looked at the floor. It was not their privilege or right to speak to such a great man without being spoken to first. "I'm very tired. I'll

retire now, and see you in the morning. Good night. Please have me woken at 8:00 a.m."

He walked up the large stairs to the second floor. The house had a central Spanish-tiled entryway, with stairways going up both sides of the spacious atrium, and a mezzanine balcony around the top. Bedrooms and baths were all off the hallway that surrounded the open atrium. There were colorful fresh flower decorations and plants of all sorts, along with local art and hangings, giving a feeling of warmth and peace. His bedroom was relatively small, with the exposed original roof timbers and plaster on the ceiling. There were Nazca drawings on the walls, and old pine and mahogany furniture scattered around the room. The floor was covered with large oriental rugs, except in some areas, which then exposed the large cypress floorboards, worn smooth from a century of feet sliding on them. Bernardo had discovered the hacienda in the late '60s. Its owners had abandoned it for many years. He loved it at first sight, even in its state of disrepair.

The view of the snow-capped Andes in the distance and the Urubamba River to the west was captivating. It had taken many years to get the place into what he and Emelia thought was suitable shape, but they had enjoyed the remodeling process, and decorating it was an endless source of entertainment. There was a large fireplace in the main room, making for an inviting living room and library. The kitchen was a separate building, attached to the back of the house with a covered walkway. All meals were prepared there, and then brought to the well-appointed dining room. Emelia had spared no expense in finding just the right tables, chairs, sideboards, silver, and handcrafted dishes and linens.

Many happy evenings had been spent in this hacienda. But now, it was just an empty building. Bernardo sighed to himself as he thought of Emelia. It was still hard to believe she was not coming in to keep him warm in his bed, as he slipped under the sheets and warm merino blankets. He closed his eyes, and fell fast asleep.

Chapter Seven

He was dreaming. He knew he was dreaming, but it was such a wonderful dream that he just let it continue. He saw Emelia, young and vibrant, her eyes shining as she ran across the university campus towards him.

"Bernardo!" She was calling his name and waving. He felt a huge smile come over his face, and his heart began to pound.

"Emelia!" he called back, and watched her body gracefully moving towards him. She was alive! How could this be? Of course, it was a dream; but so real. There was a crash off to the left. They both looked in the direction of the sound, and then abruptly, the dream was over. He awoke, eyes open wide. It was dawn, and the sun was just beginning to bring first light into his bedroom. Downstairs, he heard women's voices scolding.

"How could you be so clumsy, Alejandra, you foolish girl? Now, look what you've done! Get a broom and clean up this mess before the patron comes down for breakfast! And pray your clumsiness didn't wake him!"

A door slammed shut. *Just a dream*, he thought to himself, and sighed heavily. It was such a nice dream. They were both young, and fresh, and full of expectation. Life had just begun. His mind was fast-forwarding through so much time after university. He shook it off and swung his legs over the side of the bed. They were sore. Everything was sore nowadays. The only cure from it becoming worse was to continue his regimen of exercise. He stretched out his legs and arms, one at a time, threw back the covers and slowly got to his feet. He began his morning workout that would culminate in a brisk one-mile walk before breakfast. He had been doing the same thing every day since he had turned 40, and as such, he looked and felt at least a decade younger than the 62 he actually was.

He finished his workout, showered, and dressed in warmer clothing than the night before. Then he went downstairs for his walk. The thing he loved most about the hacienda was the silence. It was so quiet; the only noises he heard were the birds and the insects. The wind blew gently out of the west, and he took in the view of the snow-capped Andes off in the distance. He breathed in and out, savoring the clean air. In Lima, the air was so foul that he had a constant sore throat and burning in his eyes from the pollution. Here, it was just the opposite; pure, clean, crisp morning air. Even though the atmosphere was thin, it was as if his body was being purged of all the toxins of the city just by standing there and breathing in and out. He began the trek down the path from the house towards the fields below, already noticing the increase in his breathing. Even slight exertion at this altitude made an impression.

The locals were already hard at work, tending to their crops of maize, potatoes, beans, barley and wheat. The land was rich, and had been tended by the Incas and their descendants for thousands of years. He waved as he passed the people tending the fields. There were others who herded goats and sheep and of course, llamas and alpaca. He trotted up and down the worn path that had been used by the villagers here for hundreds of years. It was a rut worn into the rocky soil that was smoothed out from thousands of feet for hundreds of years. Many times he had walked it barefoot, but today it was too cold.

After about a half a mile, he turned off the path to the south and walked towards a formation of rocks. From a distance, this outcropping of stone looked like a pile of large rocks that had been pushed to the side of a field for better cultivation.

As he approached the rocks, a trained eye could see that the stones were not accidently shoved into the position they were in, but actually had a shape to them. If one looked closely enough, one could imagine the shape of a puma or cougar in a running position. He continued to the "nose" of the puma and turned right in the direction of the puma's front "paws." He continued walking for perhaps another 200 meters, scanning the surface of the ground as he walked. He saw what he was looking for ahead, slightly to his left.

Partially obscured by the tall, dry, beige grasses blowing around his legs was a round stone about the size of a manhole cover you might see on a city street. It was inscribed with intricate Incan drawings that were attractive, but to the untrained eye, would also be meaningless. The drawings were a series of circles, with Inca glyphs of animals and various gods with arrows and symbols circling around in intricate detail. He bent down and traced his finger around the inner circle, the lunar calendar to the "third month," which was actually our present-day month of February. Traditionally this is a month of offerings of great amounts of silver and gold to the gods. His finger traced outward to an arrow from the lunar marking. It pointed directly southeast.

Off in the distance, there was a stand of trees and a small stone Inca ruin. He hiked over towards the trees. *Almost there*, he thought to himself. Once within the ruins, there was a huge stone in the center of some broken walls that at one time may have been a large room. The stone seemed to almost float on the rocky surface of the floor. It was balanced on another rock underneath. *Perfectly* balanced. He jumped up on top, near the center, and walked to one end. Slowly, the stone began to dip down on the end he was standing on. It bent lower and lower until the end he was standing on touched the surface of the floor. A grinding noise of rock sliding on rock rumbled to his left.

Jumping off the rock, Bernardo ran quickly to the other end. He rolled a large round rock under the uprighted stone and into a groove that allowed the rock to lock the larger stone in place. He walked outside the broken wall and stared into an opening in the ground. It was large enough for a man to pass through if he pulled his shoulders together. Stairs made of stone led downward.

He pulled a lighter from his jacket pocket and lit the torch that lay stuck in a hole in the wall near the entrance. The pitchy end lit easily, and cast light all around as Bernardo descended the stairs. It was cold, musty, and dark. At the bottom of the stairs there was a hallway that extended for approximately fifty meters, with small trapezoid entrances off either side of the hallway that led to other rooms. He walked down the hallway, counting the entrances as he walked. At ten on the right, he held his torch up and squeezed through the narrow entrance.

The room was literally covered in gold. It seemed to explode with the light from his torch. Gold foil had been embossed onto every stone in the entire room; floor, walls, and ceiling. All around the room were objects of pottery, figures of gold and silver, cups, dishes, and disintegrating feathered capes. It was an amazing Inca museum, and had been perfectly preserved for at least a thousand years. All the rooms were similar here, and there were twenty-four of them. There was enough gold, silver, and precious stones in any of the rooms to make a man rich beyond his wildest dreams, which was exactly the case with Bernardo.

There were not many others who shared the knowledge of these hidden Inca treasure rooms. They were all over the country—not just in the Andes—as many people, especially the Spanish, had suspected. These were sanctuaries, built to sustain wealthy families in the event of natural catastrophe, war, or other emergency situations. In the name of Christianity, the Spanish conquistadors, led by Francisco Pizarro, had desecrated and pillaged the Inca Empire and its people and culture during the 1500s. They robbed the Inca of their gold and silver, and exterminating them through disease, warfare, betrayal, and slavery, until all that remained were a few artifacts. The Spaniards were so successful in their genocide that the vast portion of knowledge of this culture had vanished, leaving only clues, but no answers.

Bernardo had made this particular discovery after he had finished his training as a geologist at the university in Cuzco. He was originally interning in work for the government and some giant mining corporations during his post-graduate work in the Urubamba Valley area. Peru was rich in minerals of all sorts, but it was widely believed that the Spanish had all but depleted the gold and silver in this country. The mining companies were driven to find new sources of raw materials for export to prop up a sagging economy in Peru.

There is what is taught, and then there is legend. Legends of the surviving Quechua-speaking people of the country kept the oral tradition alive through storytelling. Many legends had survived through the time of the Spanish. But they were whispered at night and in hushed tones, in small families for generation after generation, and it was forbidden to talk of such things to anyone outside of the small villages that dotted the landscape. So there were still many secrets.

Bernardo had befriended many of the workers that were on several geological expeditions with him. These men were simple laborers with simple needs, but they needed to feed their families. They gladly would take any job that would supply them with reasonable wages, and would break their backs carrying equipment and digging holes in the ground with shovels and pickaxes. Many times the jobs were dangerous, involving explosives, for both testing and further exploration. His team's efforts rarely turned up much until a day in 1978, when a huge deposit of zinc, copper, and lead ores was discovered in an area called Huari, southeast of Cuzco, over extremely mountainous terrain.

The team had been blasting in an old, abandoned mine when they hit huge veins of a variety of ores. His company was very pleased with their efforts; not pleased enough to make him rich for his findings, but Bernardo was given a nice position as chief exploratory engineer, and a nice bump in pay. They even threw in a Land Rover for him to use. At the time, Bernardo thought he had made it to the good life. He was still young, and now he was a man of means. Yet he never lost his love or respect for the men who toiled alongside of him on these long and often dangerous journeys.

Many nights were spent outdoors; sleeping under the incredible, clear skies of the Andes. Stories were told around the fires at night. The company forbade alcohol, but since the company never came out to these areas until there was something to see, the men developed their own set of rules. Rule number ten or so on the list was that it was OK to drink Pisco, or some other alcohol, as long as you could get up the next day and work. If you couldn't, you were fired on the spot. So, after many months of travelling and working together, the men became close, and talked of women and life and love and betrayal, and occasionally of legend. An older man, Manolo, one night blurted out that there were thousands of Inca storehouses all over the areas of the countryside that used to be Peru, stretching down to Chile and up through Bolivia and Ecuador. Realizing what he had done almost immediately, and seeing the dark expressions of his compadres, he became quiet. The men changed the subject. After more Pisco and about an hour later, Bernardo asked casually about Manolo's story.

"Oh, señor, these are just stories told by old women who have nothing else to talk about. I wouldn't take them seriously," he laughed. Then the other men laughed, but without much enthusiasm. While they may have had rules for how they travelled, there were much stricter rules, unspoken rules, about what was to be talked about with anyone outside their villages.

"No, really," Bernardo pushed on. "What do you know of such places?"

Every eye of every man fell on Manolo. The message in the eyes of the men was deadly serious. Suddenly, the lighthearted atmosphere in the camp disappeared, as if all the air had just been sucked out of the tiny valley they lay in. Silence. Manolo looked nervously around the fire at the eyes looking back at him.

After a pause, he laughed and said, "Oh, señor, it's the wine talking. Just silly stories I heard as a boy. We all have heard them. They are just stories, nothing more." And with that he fell silent.

The other men nodded in agreement, and grunted and laughed. Bernardo wasn't buying it, but he also realized he was putting one of his friend's lives in jeopardy if he continued to question him. He decided to let it go.

"Yes, well, I suppose there are many of those old wives' tales, eh?" He laughed and took a swig from the bottle and passed it around. Relief flooded back into the campsite. Bernardo remained in the conversation for another twenty minutes, and then made his excuses about needing to get to sleep. He laid down on his bedroll and pulled the covers over his head. The men continued to talk for a while until one by one, the voices stopped, and silence returned. He never forgot that night, nor what happened afterward.

Two days later, as the party was exploring a deep crevice in the rocky hills around the area where they were camped, there was an "accident." Manolo, the lead guide, was being lowered down into a deep crevice in the rocks with just a rope, a pickaxe, and a swing-like seat to hold him for the dangerous descent, to take samples of the rock strata as he descended to the bottom. Of course, there was a secondary line and harness for safety, securely tied off by carabineers at the opening. But for some reason, on that particular day, with that particular person, both the main line and the safety rig came loose, and Manolo fell over two hundred meters, head and body rebounding off the crevice walls, and finally coming to a sickening thud in a pile of tangled, broken arms, legs, and neck at the bottom. It took the men six hours and well into the late evening to retrieve the remains of Manolo.

Bernardo was shocked and the men were despondent beyond words, yet no one could explain how the ropes had failed. Manolo was buried near their campsite. There was no need to fly the body out. No one, other than the men there, would ever know the difference. "These are just old wives' tales, señor," echoed through his mind.

Chapter Eight

1972

Bernardo had become fascinated by the Quechan people and their language as much as he had about the quipus, with their mysterious knots and colors. Most of the ancient information about the Inca culture, what little there was left, was in documents written in Quechua. The Quechua refer to themselves as *Runa*, "the people," as if giving claim to the rightful ownership of their culture that had been decimated by the Spanish so long ago.

Bernardo devoured everything he could find on the subject at several libraries, both public and private. Ironically, the very university that he attended was the central repository of most of the Quechan knowledge in Peru.

The Inca had four types of origin myths. In one, Tici Viracocha, of Colina de las Ventanas in <u>Paqariq Tampu,</u> sent forth his four sons and four daughters to establish a village. Along the way, <u>Sinchi Roca</u> was born to <u>Manco</u> and <u>Ocllo</u>, and Sinchi Roca is the person who finally led them to the valley of <u>Cuzco,</u> where they founded their new village. There, Manco became their leader, and became known as <u>Manco Cápac</u>.

In another origin myth, the sun god <u>Inti</u> ordered Manco Cápac and Mama Ocllo to emerge from the depths of <u>Lake Titicaca</u> and found the city of Cuzco. They traveled by means of underground caves until reaching Cuzco, where they established <u>Hurin Cuzco</u>, or the first dynasty of the Kingdom of Cuzco.

In the third origin myth, an Inca sun god told his wife that he was lonely. She proposed that he create a civilization to worship him and keep him company. He saw this as a wise plan and carried it out. The Inca were born from Lake Cuzco and populated the Andes, worshiping their sun god.

In the last origin myth, Manco Cápac, who was the son of the sun, and his sister Mama Ocllo, the daughter of the moon, were sent by the sun to look for a place to build an empire. They would know when they were at the right place by carrying a special rod with them at all times. Wherever the rod sank into the ground, this was where they were to create a new city. The rod sank into the ground in Cuzco.

The knowledge of these myths is due to oral tradition, since the Incas did not have any writing. Even less was known about the quipus. Research shows that most information on quipus is numeric, and these numbers can be read. Each cluster of knots is a digit, and there are three main types of knots: simple overhand knots; long knots consisting of an overhand knot with one or more additional turns, and figure eight knots. There also existed a fourth type of knot—a figure eight knot with an extra twist. While the majority of his research rendered a variety and quantity of information pertaining to censuses, tribute, ritual and calendric organization, genealogies, and other such matters from Incan times, Bernardo was never quite satisfied with the many scholarly conclusions.

There was a nagging suspicion in Bernardo's mind that there was more to these colorful knots than could be easily deciphered.

He was drawn to a particular quipu in the Museo Inca in Cuzco. After much negotiation with the curator, Sr. Sanchez, he was able to convince him of his sincere desire to study and examine one of the more elaborate quipus after hours, and be permitted to draw pictures. Great care had to be taken so as not to disturb the ancient artifact. Bernardo got used to wearing white cotton gloves as he carefully lifted one, and then another, and then another cord of different colors and knots and record them faithfully in a notebook. Finally after six weeks of hunching over an opened glass case in the cold museum, he thanked his friend Sr. Sanchez, and told him he would keep him informed of his work.

Bernardo had suspected that there might be a cypher in the knots of latitude and longitude, but how was that possible? Determining latitude was relatively easy in that it could be found from the altitude of the sun at noon (i.e., at its highest point) with the aid of a table giving the sun's declination for the day. Longitude was a bit more difficult, relying on occultation. The term *occultation* is most frequently used to describe those relatively frequent occasions when the Moon passes in front of a star during the course of its orbital motion around the Earth. It was widely known that the Inca people were acutely aware of the movement of the sun, the moon, and the stars. Would it be too much of a stretch, Bernardo wondered, to suggest that some of these cords and knots were actual latitudes and longitudes? He thought back to his trips with the local people, and the rumors of storehouses of great riches. They were supposedly fiction, but someone had already died in his presence from the very mention of these old tales.

He chose one of the drawings of a yellow cord. Studying the series of knots and spaces yielded little to his theory. After weeks of taking notes and studying, he went on to a blue cord. This cord was longer, with many more intricate knots. After studying the knots, they revealed two distinct groupings. Based on his knowledge of the cyphers, he discovered, to his amazement, a series of very distinct numbers—13, 28, 43, and 71, 58, 8. He found a listing of latitudes and longitudes in a world table at the library, looking up 13 degrees, 28 minutes, and 43 seconds south, and then 71 degrees, 58 minutes, and 8 seconds west. To his astonishment, they were the exact coordinates for Tambomachay, an old Inca ruin just outside of Cuzco.

"Oh my God!" Bernardo yelled in the middle of the old library, drawing stares and "Silencio!" from those around him. He slammed the big book shut and tipped over his chair as he pushed back from the large oak desk, causing yet another loud noise in the cavernous library. Ignoring the glares of other students, he walked as swiftly as he could to the exit, beaming from ear to ear. What else could be on that quipu?

Soon he returned to the library with many more deciphered latitudes and longitudes. Some revealed little, but one in particular caught his attention. The location was in the Sacred Valley, near Yucay. After going to the local public records office, he located an old topographical map of the exact area he was looking for, and set out first on motorcycle, and then on foot to find the coordinates:

13 degrees, 18 minutes, 14.6 seconds south, and 72 degrees, 4 minutes, and 34.3 seconds west. The steep terrain was nestled among terraced fields. Nearby was a small abandoned farmhouse. He leaned his motorcycle against the old farmhouse, and set out on foot towards the coordinates. Bernardo scanned the fields and rocks in every direction, but saw nothing. He continued heading west. Suddenly, as if emerging from the soil and grass, a large rock appeared in the distance. As he got closer, he noticed it had the odd shape of a panther, "running" towards the north. Instinctively, he turned and followed in a straight line from the rock. After a hundred yards or so, there appeared to be another outcropping of stones in the high grass. Almost completely buried in the dirt and grass was a large, circular stone. After brushing away the dirt and small plants, he recognized immediately that it was an Incan calendar, with a slightly raised triangle of metal. It cast its shadow to a different direction based on the height of the sun, today pointing northwest. After a short period of walking, he found another outcropping of rocks. His heart was pounding with excitement. Could this be his long-sought discovery, after all these years of study?

At first glance, there wasn't much to see. Several large rocks, carefully fit together, lay in an embankment. In front of the stones was a very large stone, leaning almost at a perfect balancing point on top of another perfectly shaped cylindrical stone. He climbed atop the rock and walked up the incline. The stone began to tip downwards. As it did, the stones in the embankment behind him made a slight shifting sound, rock against rock, but not grinding exactly; more smooth in nature. He turned to look over his shoulder and noticed that a large stone had started to slide to one side of the embankment. In his shock, he fell backwards towards the embankment, and the large rock that had been moving right, now moved left and closed the embankment. An opening? To what? And where?

He climbed up again onto what he later called the balancing rock, and walked to the other end, looking over his shoulder. A door, clearly a door, opened behind him! When he looked down at the upending side of the balancing rock, he noticed two round rocks, the size of softballs, on either side. They were lying in a U-shaped track of some kind from left to right. It appeared to his engineering mind that if he had time to jump off the rock and quickly push the two round rocks into the center of the track, it would keep the balancing rock in the "open" position. He jumped off and ran to the round stones. They were very heavy. He grabbed moss and smeared the track and pushed first one, and then the other into the middle, just as the balancing stone was starting to move back to its original position. It was held fast in place by the round rocks.

He gazed at the opening behind him, and into the darkness within. Cold air was drifting out of the hole that was just big enough for a small man to fit through. He shuddered from his discovery. *Should I go in? What if I get stuck? No one would ever find me.* He walked towards the opening. Just inside, on a wall, was a short pole with what appeared to be pitch on the end. He touched it. It was sticky and thick. He brought it out into the light, found a lighter in his pocket, and held it under the pitchy end. It lit within seconds, throwing off black smoke. *Might as well take a look,* he thought, shivering slightly, and held the primitive light towards the opening. There was enough light to expose a stone stairway descending into the ground. Along the way he could make out vague images of other pitch torches stuck into the walls of the stairway. He had to go. Squeezing through the narrow entrance, he slowly descended the stone stairs, lighting other pitch torches along the walls as he went. The stairway became very bright. The walls and ceiling were covered with what appeared to be a type of metal, giving off a reflective golden light. He reached out and tapped the wall with his fingernail. It *was* metal; in fact, not just any metal. He scratched it with his fingernail. It was gold foil. The further down he went and the more torches he lit, the more illuminated the hallways below became. Bernardo had to continuously remind himself to breathe. He was incredulous. The steps finally ended approximately thirty meters from the top. He turned around and could see the opening and sunlight at the top of the stone stairs. He was more interested in what lay ahead. He began a ritual of moving along, lighting another pitch light, and moving cautiously further. A large hallway extended into the darkness. He reached the first room after about ten meters down the hallway. It had a trapezoid-shaped doorway, typical of the Incas, to prevent collapse from earthquakes. He poked his torch inside, and the entire room light up. Floors, walls, and ceiling were all covered in gold. He was so astonished at the sight, he almost dropped the torch. Then he noticed the artifacts in the room—great thrones and other furniture, pottery, capes of feathers, idols of the gods made in gold and silver. Wooden boxes were overflowing with precious stones. Tears began streaming down his face. He had found it. The lost storehouse of the Incas! He withdrew from the room and went down the hallway to room after room of similar marvels. He stopped at 18. There were more.

Suddenly, Bernardo became terrified. He retreated backwards to the stairs, extinguishing the torches as he went until he reached the bottom of the stairway. He was out of breath, although oddly, the air inside this large chamber seemed fresh.

When he reached the top of the steps, he blew out the last torch, replacing it where he had found it. He took some moss and mud and smeared the paths of the round rocks to return them to their original positions. Jumping on the end of the upended large balancing rock, he moved it slightly, then jumped off. The round rocks were easily moved back to their original positions as the balancing stone gently moved on its pivot towards the open door, which slowly slid shut with hardly a sound.

Bernardo sat down on the grass and tried to take in what he had just discovered. Although it was a cool afternoon, he was covered with sweat and shaking violently. He comforted himself by putting his arms around himself as he rocked back and forth, weeping. His own private museum! Wealth beyond measure had just become his, and yet, he could tell no one.

Almost a mile away, a very young officer in the Peruvian Army focused a very strong pair of binoculars on Bernardo. He smirked as he lowered the glasses. *So he figured it out*, he thought to himself. He would have to tell the others, of course, but good for him! Sergeant Victor de la Hoya scribbled a few notes, put them in his uniform pocket, and left Yucay, unnoticed.

Chapter Nine - Victor

1959

Victor de la Hoya grew up in a very poor area of Lima called Rímac. His mother and father had left the hills of the Andes in search of a better life, only to find that life in the city was even worse. It was hard to find jobs, and with no education to speak of, the jobs they could find were barely enough to make ends meet. Many nights Victor and his brothers and sisters went without any food. His father would come home drunk. His parents would fight. Sometimes he would hit his mother. It made all the kids fearful of their father turning his wrath on them, so they laid very still. They were crowded together in the two-room apartment with nothing to sleep on but old rags and pieces of blankets. Each night, Victor would pray for a miracle to happen, and wipe away his tears with his dirty hands. Each day, a battle in the streets of Rímac was waiting for him. Children of all ages roamed the streets for something to eat, something to steal, someone to pick a fight with. It was their only release from the nightmare of living in this densely populated, filthy hellhole. Victor was unusually tall for his age, and as such, developed a reputation of winning more fights than he lost. When it came to stealing from the local merchants, he was fearless, often coming home with some fruit or vegetables from the local mercado. His mother never asked questions; they needed the food to survive. But somewhere in his hardening heart, Victor knew his mother was disappointed in him, which made him feel all the more guilty and angry. Why wouldn't this God that he prayed to answer his prayers?

His mother dragged all the children to Mass every Wednesday and Sunday at Nuestra Señora de la Consolación (Our Lady of Consolation), where they prayed, and listened to a strange language called Latin from the priest, and lit candles. Occasionally, there was bread and food given to the poor, usually near the holidays, when summer was bearing down on Peru and making the church and their tiny bedroom even more hot and unbearable than normal. Victor began to give up hope. He had gone to Mass, he had gone to confession, he had prayed as hard as he could, but no miracles occurred.

Oddly enough, on his tenth birthday, which happened to fall on a Sunday, one of the nuns approached Señora de la Hoya after Mass, and whispered something quietly to her. Victor studied his mother's face intently. Her eyes flew up to the sky; she forgot herself and began hugging the nun and yelling: "Gracias a Dios! Gracias Jesús!" over and over again. She bent down to Victor, took his face in both hands, tears streaming down her face, and said, "God has answered your prayers! You have been chosen by Sister Magdalena to go to school here and live in the dormitory with other boys. She feels you have been called by God to become a priest!"

Victor was stunned. He felt as if the wind had been knocked out of him. For a long moment he stared at his mother's face, and felt as if he would cry himself. Was this possible? Yet there was the nun, smiling down at him and reaching out to take his hand. Now? Right now?

"But, Mother," Victor stammered, "what about the rest of the family? How can this be?"

His mother looked sternly at him, and said in the strongest voice he had ever heard her use, "Victor de la Hoya, God given you a gift that cannot be explained. You are not to question such things. This is truly a miracle. Do not mock your Father in Heaven by questioning Him. Do you understand me?"

Victor nodded his head, unable to speak. He took the nun's hand and, after waving a faint good-bye to his mother and brothers and sisters, he was led back towards the church. He would never see any of them ever again.

1966

Victor de la Hoya was an outstanding student. He did well in all his classes, and was being groomed. He knew that after completing high school he would be sent to a seminary to study to become a priest. He rarely was allowed outside the gates of the school compound. Rímac, he was told by his fellow students and teachers alike, was a dangerous place, which always amused Victor. He now had fresh uniforms to wear, a bathroom with a shower to use whenever he liked—with hot water! He ate three meals a day, and ate well; after praying, of course. He did his best to blend in with his fellow students, never wanting them to know where he came from. He secretly longed to see his family, but he was strictly forbidden to leave the grounds without permission, which was often requested, but never approved. He did not understand, but he did know that this life was far better than he had ever asked or imagined, and would not risk that for anything or anyone.

Still, his longing to see his mother and family after all these years tugged at his heart. He was allowed to receive letters from his mother; unfortunately, she was illiterate, and had to have a friend write them to Victor and leave them at the church. Life had not gone well for the rest of the de la Hoya family. His father had gone to prison as a result of a drunken brawl in the streets, where he had cut another man's throat with a shard of a broken beer bottle. His mother, brothers, and sisters had to move to the hills of Lima where they lived in abject poverty: no running water, no electricity, a cardboard box with a blue tarp roof for a house. The floor was dusty and dry dirt in the summer, and muddy and mixed with urine and feces in the winter, because it was too cold to go outside. Their stove was an open fire outside the box. Most of the time they had no food. His sisters had turned to prostitution to make ends meet, and Maria was now pregnant with someone's child for the second time in two years. More mouths to feed, more desperation to console them. His brothers had become criminals and ran with gangs that robbed people at night, feeding their addictions during the day.

Guilt washed over Victor every time he ate a full meal, or used a bar of soap, or drank clean water. He would push those feelings as far down as they could go, only allowing them to surface as anger at God. What kind of God could allow this to happen to his family? He asked many of the brothers and priests, but never got a satisfactory answer. He often wondered why the church, with all its wealth and power, never seemed to help those with less. Wasn't that the very thing Jesus had preached in the Sermon on the Mount?

One night, Victor decided he had to visit his mother and family. He snuck out of the compound after vespers, and headed on foot to the hills of Lima. At first there were cement steps leading up the hill. After climbing for several hundred meters, the steps ended, and the paths began. The further up he went, the more pathetic the housing became until at the very end, there was nothing but barren shacks of cardboard and wood and plastic. Small fires burnt everywhere for heat or cooking, and the smell of human misery was everywhere. He knew approximately where his mother might be living. From time to time, he would stop someone and ask for his mother. Did they know her, or where she lived? Most of the time he received strange stares and no comment. What was this fancy-pants schoolboy doing roaming around in this place? Surely he must be crazy, or after someone.

Victor came across a group of boys, most of whom were about his age, but aged beyond their years. They came towards him, laughing and joking about how perhaps he taken a wrong turn somewhere. Victor instinctively knew this was trouble. He had not forgotten his street smarts even after all this time. There were four of them. As they approached him, two went to his left, one towards his front, and the other to his right.

"Oye, chico, are you lost or something?" said one, as he reached into his pocket. Victor considered his situation. He could probably take two or three of them, but not all four. He glanced around in the dark for something to protect himself with. Nearby was the beginning of some sort of homemade cement structure with rebar sticking up in the air. The gang all drew closer. The boy in front of him pulled a knife out of his pocket and flipped it open.

"We'd like to welcome you to our neighborhood, señor, but first we will need you to give us your watch and your money, and maybe that nice jacket you're wearing too, if it's okay with you…"

All the others laughed and moved in for the attack. Victor did not hesitate. He kicked the knife boy squarely in the balls, turned and hit the two guys behind him with a high round kick, and dove for the rebar next to him.

He grabbed the hard piece of steel and yanked. It stayed stuck in the cement. Boy number four was moving towards him. He crawled quickly over to knife boy, who was at that time bent over in agony. Victor found the knife, turned, and as his final attacker charged, caught him squarely in the abdomen, plunging the knife all the way until his hand hit his chest. Blood began to gush out of the wound. He pulled the knife out as the boy went down, grabbing his stomach.

Victor flashed the knife at the other two, who were getting up from their kicks in the face to attack again.

"All right, you fuckers!" Victor shouted. "Which of you is next?"

It appeared the popular consensus was not only surprise at being outmaneuvered, but also to live another day. They turned and ran, leaving their friend to bleed out on the muddy path.

Victor gazed down at the boy groaning in agony. It was a lethal wound. Victor dropped the knife and began to make his way down the muddy path to the stairs.

He found his way home, cleaned his clothes, took a shower, and fell into bed, only to be surprised a few hours later by a priest shaking his shoulder gently.

"Victor. The police have come here. They say they have evidence that you have killed someone. A boy, up in the hills. Is this true?"

Victor sat straight up in bed. How did they know? The priest and Victor both looked down at the muddy and blood-spattered boots under his bed at the same time.

Damn, thought Victor. *I'm screwed.*

The magistrate who tried the case was clearly unsympathetic to Victor. The cast of witnesses included the remaining three boys from that night, the murder weapon with his bloody fingerprints on it, and the solemn testimony from the boys and their families that he was looking for trouble that night, and they were just trying to help him find his mother. Why he acted in such a hostile manner was unknown to them. After all, they were just trying to help a boy find his family. The magistrate knew the boys and the gang they ran with. He knew they were lying, and no doubt had started the fight. And yet there was a dead boy, nonetheless. Justice had to be served. Many priests and nuns had begged him for mercy on Victor's behalf. At his sentencing, Victor was given a very simple choice: twenty years in prison, or immediately entering the Peruvian Army. A sadder, but wiser Victor de la Hoya lived to see another day, and a glorious career in the Peruvian military.

1971

Victor adjusted to life in the military very well. Of course, the incentive of not spending twenty years in Miguel Castro Prison in San Juan de Lurigancho (one of the most notorious, and vicious prisons in Lima to spend a day in, let alone twenty years) made it more of an opportunity to achieve, than to fail. Victor rose through the ranks to become a young sergeant at the age of 22. He was stationed in a remote military outpost in Arequipa. Fortunately for Victor, and other members of the Peruvian Army, a coup d'état by Juan Velasco Alvarado left the military in a very strong position to control the country, controlling the oil and other natural resources of Peru, and sending President Fernando Belaúnde into exile.

Victor was often used by the army as an escort for local and national dignitaries, primarily because of his education, intelligence, and good manners, transporting important men from one place to another. He was never told what the mission was. It was merely a matter of picking up person "A" at this airport, and transporting him to this place "B" at a specific time. He never questioned his orders, and never spoke a word to his "guests" unless he was spoken to. One man, a powerful politician that he recognized from the newspapers, Sr. Alberto Fujimori, was often his passenger. He was a Peruvian of Japanese descent, educated mostly in the United States, but spoke little as he was shuttled back and forth by Sergeant Victor de la Hoya from one important government meeting to another.

As he was driving his familiar passenger to the airport one day, Sr. Fujimori said to Victor, "You have been faithful in driving me and protecting me in all manner of places and circumstances, Sergeant. I want you to know how much I appreciate your dedication. Here..." He handed something to Victor from the rear of the car. Victor reached out and received whatever it was that this strange Japanese man was handing him. He figured it was a tip. It was not. It was a small figurine of a golden condor; a pin to attach to clothing.

"Wear this whenever you are in your civilian clothes, Sergeant. It will protect you, and will provide, shall I say, a level of comfort that perhaps you are not used to. Someone will contact you soon to let you know more about what this means. For now, please accept this gift as a token of my appreciation."

Victor accepted the piece of jewelry, and stuffed it in his upper left pocket.

"Thank you, Sr. Fujimori," he said with as much enthusiasm as he could muster. Most men of this stature saw people like him as invisible servants.

"If you do as we ask of you, Sergeant, many more riches and success will come to you. You have my word on that." With those final words, as they arrived at the airport, Sr. Fujimori stepped out of the car, and Victor de la Hoya would not see this man again for another two decades, when he would become President of Peru.

Chapter Ten

Present Day

Bernardo was looking for a particular artifact. One he had left behind in this room, number 10 right, several years ago. It was a possible clue within a clue. He held his torch higher, and saw the object he was looking for hanging on one of the walls. To the untrained eye, it appeared almost to be a necklace, with one very long string suspending various other strings of yellow, red, blue and white that hung down against the gold-plated wall. Each attached string had a variety of lengths and a series of elaborate knots, the quipu. Hypotheses abounded, but the "language" of the Inca Empire that was a system of different knots tied in strings attached to a longer cord was still largely a mystery. The strings' different colors may have had encoded information in the choice of the colors themselves. There was some written evidence from the Spanish that quipus encoded census data, accounting figures and calculations, as well as stories.

Some were suspected to be census data of the particular tribe; some others, information. Tragically, most of the quipus, and all of the Incas, or Tawantinsuyu, had been murdered and destroyed by the Spanish. Through a great deal of time, trouble, and research with the locals, and having a good working knowledge of Quechua, Bernardo was able to "translate" one of the blue knotted cords on this ornately decorated quipu. The one that Bernardo had decoded held very valuable information; the location of various storehouses, like the one he was standing in. It was not enough to just know the generalized location given through the knots, but also how to read the stone symbols that were usually nearby the storehouses, and the calendar stones that also pointed the way. The rest, frankly, was dumb luck and timing. Part of the information stored on his thumb drive was the latitude and longitude settings deciphered from this cord for the other storehouses. Right now, he needed to check his work.

Bernardo's "find" in the Andes had not attracted much attention for one reason. He had told no one, not even Emelia. He realized that the significance of what he had found was both a blessing and a curse. He was blessed beyond measure to know that his people were wiser than the Spaniards had ever given them credit for, and of course, the wealth that came with the find was also a blessing. Millions and millions of soles worth of gold in just one room! The curse? How do you hide millions and millions of soles worth of gold, silver, and precious stones? If word ever got out, the plunder and mayhem for the riches and artifacts would destroy it all, and probably him along with it. He felt the weight of an entire civilization on his shoulders. For over two years, he did absolutely nothing but study. He just thought about what it was like to suddenly be wealthy beyond measure. He found that his only worry in life suddenly was, ironically, life. *His* life, and the life of his wife.

He devoured all there was to know about the quipu, which was surprisingly very little. Some of the world's best mathematicians, encryption specialists, glyphers, and Inca scholars had worked on deciphering the "talking knots," as they were sometimes called. One thing he had learned was that parts of the quipu were actually calculations and tabulations of everything from taxes to crop production. Colors and sequences of colors also had significance. For reasons Bernardo had never understood, the blue thread on the quipu he'd studied for over three years had held his attention the most. This single blue thread that he had partially decoded through years of study, questioning experts, and his own research on the Internet had brought him to his first find. In the end, it was a series of ornate knots that translated into decimals and then numbers, uncannily accurate numbers. After much further research, they revealed, to his astonishment, exact longitude and latitude marks, 13°18'34.28"S and 72°05'03.81"W. Using his GPS, he found at that exact spot the "Puma" rock outcropping.

The rest, as they say, was history. His research had revealed more. Yucay, roughly translated from its original Spanish, meant "deceit," and was the original site of the last of the rebel Vilcabamba (Quechan for "sacred valley," or "valley of the gods") Inca warrior chiefs, Sauri Túpac, or Túpac Amaru. In the mid-1500s he had amassed a rebel force of over 100,000 warriors to take a stand against the conquistadores, but to no avail. The Spanish, with their pistols, rifles, and cannon, easily overwhelmed Sauri Túpac and his men, and slaughtered them as they retreated into the jungles to the south. The city of deceit. It seemed like poetic justice to Bernardo.

Years after his find, Bernardo brought several precious stones to his home not far away. One stone was an emerald, the size of a medium-sized lime. It was not finely faceted or polished, but he imagined it was clearly worth a great deal of money. He would take it to Columbia later that year and claim to have found it on an expedition. When it was finally weighed and valued, the 150-carat rough emerald fetched over 350,000 soles. One stone! Actually, it had been one of the smaller ones. Another stone was set in a ruby ring, encased in pure gold, which he presented to his wife on their anniversary. It seemed like a good idea at the time; unfortunately, Bernardo underestimated the knowledge and curiosity of his wife. She practically fainted when she took the ring out of the box; initially thrilled, but then came the questions.

"Bernardo, how can you afford such a precious piece of jewelry?" "Where did you find this?" "I've never seen this kind of artistry before," and so on. It became inevitable that he had to tell Emelia the truth. He swore her to secrecy, and to her credit, although she could hardly believe what her husband had told her, and later shown her, she never said a word about it. Ever.

The curse continued. After carefully selling to discreet buyers all over South America for several years, he slowly was being transformed from Bernardo the geologist, to Bernardo the exporter of fine precious stones and metals. After four years, he resigned his position with the mining company, claiming he had found a new position with another company. There was the mounting problem of what to do with all the money he had amassed. Putting it in the bank was too obvious, and begged the government to ask very serious questions about the origins of such wealth. Bringing it back through customs was becoming more and more difficult because of the amounts of cash. He was attracting attention, the last thing he wanted to do. He had stashed over a million soles in his hacienda in Yucay. He had more in plastic bags buried within the very storehouses the wealth had originated from.

And so, ironically, the storehouses became his own private banks, with "branches" in different parts of the country in various storehouses he had discovered over the years. Still, with all the measures he had taken to remain silent and not be followed, he was inevitably found out. Thankfully, it did not end as he had feared. One night, as he was heading home by taxi in Lima, he got out of the cab and paid his fare. The driver made eye contact, and handed him an object wrapped in paper.

"I was told to give this to you," he said, and before Bernardo could open his mouth to say, "By whom?" the cab sped off into the foggy evening. He unwrapped the paper, and inside was a small, golden condor, no bigger than the size of a 5-sole coin. There were no markings of any kind on it. The paper it had been wrapped in had writing on the inside. It said, "You're not alone. Meet me at the Plaza de Armas in downtown Lima at 23:00 tomorrow. I'll be standing in the middle doorway of the cathedral." And a simple signature, "Victor." And so, with some fear, the following evening he met Victor de la Hoya for the first time.

Victor, who was at the time only a ranking officer in the Peruvian Army, introduced himself the next evening with a smile and a warm handshake. They went for coffee in a small shop around the corner. They were in turn led to a back room where there was privacy; only a small table and two chairs. Coffee was served with some small sandwiches, and then silence.

"You must be very curious about why I have contacted you, no?" said Victor.

Bernardo could only nod his head. He was terrified. Meeting with a member of the military and speaking about a thing he had vowed he would never discuss with anyone was dangerous. There was much to lose; perhaps his freedom, or something worse. And yet, there was something about this man who smiled and spoke softly, with ease and confidence, that led Bernardo to believe that perhaps he could be trusted. It seemed this man knew a great deal about him already. He noticed the golden condor on the lapel of his jacket. It was exactly like the one he had received the night before.

"You're no doubt thinking that I'm here to arrest you, or worse. Relax, my friend; we have much to discuss. I'll talk, you will listen, and I can promise you that by the end of our talk, you will know that this night, your life will be forever changed...or, it will end."

Victor then began to tell him about *Los Cóndores de Oro.* Bernardo listened, spellbound, while Victor told him that there were many men, just like him, who had discovered the secrets of the quipu, and they were spread all over South America, not just in Peru. Like it or not, Bernardo had become a part of an organization of men who would either embrace him, or kill him, and that choice would be made this evening. Bernardo shuddered slightly at the last comment, but leaned forward to listen even more intently. There were no requirements other than secrecy, and participation in annual meetings. They met in secret, in places that would not be noticed by anyone who mattered. Sometimes they met in other countries, sometimes in the recesses of Peru.

The meetings were short, and the agenda normally the same; manipulation of politicians, power, and money. These men controlled more of the governments of the southern hemisphere and parts of Europe, and even the United States, than Bernardo had even dared to imagine. The accrued wealth of these men exceeded the oil-rich Arabian countries in the Far East as well as much of Northern Asia. Los Cóndores de Oro was a name whispered by legend throughout the southern hemisphere. It was rumored that there was, in fact, a group of men who controlled the world; and then of course, laughed about, and dismissed. How could such a thing be? Were there not governments that were elected by the people? Even the dictatorships and the armies that backed them could not be intimidated by such a group. How could any group of men be that powerful? It was, of course, very possible; but people wanted desperately to believe that their destinies, their fates, and their decisions were actually their own, not controlled by someone else. These stories could only be those of paranoid groups who saw conspiracies all around them. Insanity. Silliness. Which was just the way the "group" liked it.

When Victor was finally finished talking, he sat back, and said casually, "Any questions?"

Bernardo's head was swimming. There was no doubt in his mind that what he had been told was the absolute truth. No one could have made this up; it was too elaborate a scheme to simply defraud him of his money.

"No," he said, as firmly as he could muster.

"Good," said his new friend. "So, it would be safe for me to tell our group you have accepted their offer?" he said in a matter-of-fact manner.

"Yes!" Bernardo almost shouted. He was so nervous he wanted to make sure there was no doubt. "Actually," he said, thinking about the conversation, "I do have one question."

Victor leaned forward and said, "And that would be?"

Bernardo thought for a moment about how to compose the question. "How did you find out about me? I thought I had covered all my tracks."

"Oh, my friend," he laughed softly, "you did a great job! Better than most. You simply forgot about one thing." He let the sentence hang in the air.

"And that was?" asked Bernardo, wondering what in the world it could possibly have been.

"You remember Señor Sanchez, the professor of history and curator you approached a few years ago?"

"Yes," he said haltingly.

"Señor Sanchez noticed your focus on the blue cords and knots, and your obvious wealth of knowledge of the quipus. He, of course, is one of us, and he activated a network that has followed you ever since. What we learned about you for the two years we have watched you is that you're a man of honor and integrity. You have a great love of your country, and its history, and people, and you know how to keep your mouth shut. You're industrious, intelligent, and generous. It was these things that not only saved your life, and made you reasonably rich, but also caused this meeting to happen tonight. Does that answer your question, amigo?" He laughed a small laugh of amusement.

Bernardo was astonished. It only confirmed what he had thought earlier. The whole scene seemed surreal to him. It appeared to him suddenly that his life of secrecy had been totally exposed, observed, and calculated from nearly start to finish. It was both unnerving and exhilarating.

"Oh," was the only thing Bernardo could think of to say. Victor rose from the table, preparing to leave. Bernardo hurriedly got to his feet as well.

"Well, my new friend, we will be in contact with you in the near future. Until then, please feel free to call upon me at any time to help with any 'difficulties' you may run into. Think of it this way; you now have behind you more power than most men could ever even imagine. It's being entrusted to you to use wisely."

He handed him a card, and then moved towards the door. "Oh," he said over his shoulder as he walked out a side door, "say hello to Emelia for me, won't you?" And he shut the door behind him.

The card in his hand simply had Victor's name and a telephone number on it. Bernardo hailed a cab, and directed the driver to his home. His head was spinning. He felt nauseous and high at the same time. It all seemed like a dream. As the empty streets rushed by, he looked out the front windshield and then at the dashboard of the cab from the rear seat. Stuck into the fake leather dashboard, faded from years of driving thousands of kilometers, was a small golden condor.

CHAPTER ELEVEN - EMELIA

1966

Emelia Mercedes Sanchez Podera finished high school early in Lima. She was nearly the top student in her class, excelling in almost every subject she undertook. She had always wanted to become a lawyer, but her father discouraged such a ridiculous idea. He respected her enough to allow her to go to university, but only until she could find herself a suitable husband. Both Jorge and Maria agreed upon that, although her mother secretly wished for her to become a doctor. Such things were unheard of in the 1960s in Peru, although as the American songwriter Bob Dylan had once said, "The times they are a-changin'." And indeed they were; as in the United States, this was a time of great turmoil in Peru.

As President Belaúnde took office in 1963, with the help of General Velasco and the military, there were large groups of peasants who forcefully took over areas of land, sometimes violently, against the Patron landowners. More radical groups, Cuban inspired, also saw the growing rural ferment as an opportunity to begin armed revolution in the countryside. Squatter cities and villages sprang up in areas where only the rich and privileged had once thrived. Such was the case with her beloved Ancón and its surrounding areas, and thus began the decline of the area for tourism and vacationing. Ambitious land reform in the 1960s by the government seemed to have broken the back of the old landed estates. Social tensions unleashed by the new government's first attempts at reform prompted a military coup led by General Juan Velasco himself. To everybody's surprise, the Velasco government threw its weight behind the new reforms. It nationalized the oil wells of the International Petroleum Company, a subsidiary of Standard Oil of New Jersey. Most importantly, it enacted a sweeping agrarian reform, which abolished the old Andean estates, as well as newer coastal plantations. The peasants still depended on the estates for grazing land and functioned as service tenants—a form of pre-capitalist production. The agrarian reform hardly affected the surrounding countryside in the Urubamba Valley at all. While the peasants had the right to become owners of the land they resided on, they had to pay for it. As a consequence, the plantation owner was able to keep back the best land for himself.

When Velasco was overthrown by another military coup that implemented some counter-reforms, the general direction of Peruvian politics took a sharp left turn. Eventually, Alan Garcia became president. He was the candidate of the APRA party, a left-wing nationalist formation that rejected socialism. Among the strongest of the opposition during this period was a Marxist group commonly known as "The Shining Path," founded by former university philosophy professor Abimael Guzmán.

Between 1973 and 1975, Shining Path members gained control of the student councils in the Universities of Huancayo and La Cantuta, and developed a significant presence in the National University of Engineering in Lima and the National University of San Marcos, the oldest university in the Americas. Some time later, it lost many student elections in the universities, including Guzmán's Universito of San Cristóbal of Huamanga. It decided to abandon recruiting at the universities and reconsolidate. It was this group and many splinter groups that grew in power during the 1980s, particularly in the Andean highlands. They brought to trial and killed managers of the state-controlled farming collectives and well-to-do merchants, who were unpopular with poor rural dwellers. These actions caused the peasantry of many Peruvian villages to express some sympathy for the Shining Path, especially in the impoverished and neglected regions of Ayacucho, Apurímac, and Huancavelica. At times, the civilian population of small, neglected towns participated in such popular trials, especially when the victims of the trials were widely disliked.

It was during this tumultuous time in her country's history that Emelia chose to attend the National University of San Antonio Abad near her home in Cuzco. There she began her studies in 1964, focusing on politics more and more as the years went by. It was popular on campus to be involved in Socialist clubs and activities, much to the dismay of her parents, who disapproved of her ever-increasing leftist viewpoints. Emelia would often spend weekends in the hillsides around Cuzco talking with the paramilitary MIR. She became more and more sympathetic to the plight of the people of the countryside, who were being exploited by the rich landowners. Emelia was well known by many of the revolutionaries in the area and as such, was able to move freely among the villages without fear of being questioned, or worse, killed. She was admired for her compassion and interest in the people, and it was not uncommon for her to contribute money, food, and clothing to the "movement" when she could. She had made it clear to the men that she was there to help, but not to take up arms.

Emelia had grown into an extremely attractive young woman. While she possessed many of the features of the indigenous people of the Cuzco area, her father's contribution, she also was lighter skinned and had some European features from her mother's side, allowing her to be somewhat taller than usual, with high cheekbones and an uncharacteristically thin nose and lips. Her long brown hair was usually tied back behind her with a scarf, and she dressed very simply in traditional skirts and blouses. Her figure was slender, but attractively proportioned. She knew she was pretty, but was hardly ever approached by any of the young men at the university. Perhaps it was her aloofness and confidence that kept them away. Certainly, it was not that she was shy. Emelia was pleasant and polite to all she met, and her beautiful smile lit up her face with a natural glow that most people she met felt disarmed by. And yet, she was lonely.

There had always been men who had made advances to her, even at a younger age, but they were mostly crude and unrefined. She rebuffed them easily by simply dismissing them with a frown, a fiery look in her eyes, and a flip of her hair that was easily understood by any man of whom she disapproved. Words were rarely necessary. Her best friend in university, Rosario, told her she needed to relax a bit more.

"At least give them a chance," she would say. "Don't you want men to notice you? Don't you want to find a rich husband?" She always encouraged Emelia to wear more makeup and use lipstick. Rosario had lots of male friends. They buzzed around her like bees. For Emelia, they were mostly annoyances. They seemed so immature and unaware of what was going on around them. They, like her, were from privileged families that had no interest in the plights of the people living around them. As far as they were concerned, the people were invisible. They were there to serve, nothing more.

In her second year, Emelia took a course on the history of the Inca people. It was a course that literally came alive because, after studying for several weeks, the class would often pile into buses and travel to the Inca ruins that surrounded the countryside. The closest and perhaps most visited of these sites was Sacsahuamán. The ruins were spectacular, with stone walls of rocks, sometimes several stories high, weighing ridiculous amounts, intricately fitted together with perfection and forming virtually impenetrable walls. On one side of the ruins there were natural curved rocks, where many of the local children and of course, the tourists, came. These curved rocks formed natural slides that could drop as much as 13 meters. It was at this spot, on a bright sunny day in November, that Emelia fell in love.

There was a group of young men, one in particular whom she recognized from her classes, that were sliding down the slides, and then making the perilous climb back up to do it all over again. Rosario was first around the corner to the area where the slides were, followed closely by Emelia.

They were chatting about the class and the Incan design of the fortress, taking field notes for their class, until they saw the young men. Both groups fell silent momentarily. One young man had just come to a crashing heap at the bottom of the slide, practically at Emelia's feet. Everyone laughed. The young man got up quickly and pretended not to be injured; after all, he was in the presence of two beautiful women. It would be bad form to whine about the scrapes on his elbows and arms that he had used as brakes to stop his fall. Emelia looked at the handsome man as he brushed the dust off himself and then noticed the blood on his elbows and hands.

"Oh, you're hurt!" she said, stepping forward to help him up. Bernardo avoided the outstretched hand. He couldn't allow his friends to see him helped by a woman, even a beautiful woman.

"No, no thank you." He gestured at her, waving her off. "It's just a scratch," he said, and he painfully got to his feet.

"I wouldn't call all that blood dripping down your arm a scratch," Emelia said, fire in her eyes; but this time of a different sort. "Here, let me help you." She reached behind her neck and untied the scarf that held her long brown hair back, shook her head slightly, and handed him the scarf.

Bernardo accepted the gesture. "But this will ruin your scarf. Are you sure?"

She stepped closer to him with a frustrated look on her face and took the scarf back from him, grabbed his arm, and began to dab at the blood. Men could be so stubborn! "No," she said, looking him in the eyes, and then down to his injured elbow. "This is nothing. Now please, let me help you." He winced as she dabbed at the cut. "Oh, I'm sorry," she said. "Does that hurt?"

"No," he said, ignoring the pain in his arm. He was too enamored with this beautiful young woman attending to him. It was as if the rest of the world had simply vanished, and it was just the two of them talking. Their friends were forgotten. He could hear voices, but all he could do was see this woman and her scarf.

"I'm Emelia," she said.

"Pleased to meet you, Emelia, and uh, thanks for your help. It really isn't necessary." She held his arm tighter and tied the scarf around the wound on his elbow.

"There," she said with finality. "That should stop the bleeding; but you really should clean that up when you go home, you know?"

"Yes, yes I will," said Bernardo.

"Do you have a name?" She looked straight into his eyes. He noticed the fire and upturned eyebrow, a small smile creeping across her face.

"Oh, uh, of course," he stammered out. *What a fool I must seem!* he thought to himself. "Yes, I'm sorry, it's Bernardo."

"Well, Bernardo, it's nice to have met you," she said, extending her hand to him.

He awkwardly grabbed her hand with both of his and said, "Yes, you too, Emelia....and uh, thank you for your nursing!" They both laughed nervously, and then noticed that their hands had lingered together longer than either of them had intended. It was as if they didn't want to let go.

"Emelia, come on! We need to go!" shouted Rosario. They both snapped back in an instant and pulled back their hands.

"I have to go. Nice to have met you, Bernardo." She smiled at him.

Bernardo panicked; he couldn't just let her go. "Uh, wait... where are you from? Here in Cuzco?" he asked.

"Yes, I live here and go to the University at San Antonio Abad. You should know; you're in my history class!" she yelled to him as she ran towards her friend.

"I am?" said Bernardo, totally dumbfounded.

"Ciao!" was all he heard, and then the two women ran around the edge of the rocks.

His friends called to him and came down the slide, harassing him mercilessly: "Oh, Bernardo, you got it bad!" "Bernardo, does your little arm feel better now?" "Oh, Bernardo, you are so strong and handsome!" He laughed with them as they shoved each other playfully.

"Let's do it one more time!" said one of his friends, and they scrambled up the rocks again to go on the slides one more time before they left.

"Maybe I should go headfirst," said Alberto. "I could half-kill myself and get the other one to take off her blouse to fix my head!" Bernardo shoved his friend down the slide.

"Shut up, you idiot!" he laughed. *Emelia,* Bernardo thought to himself. *I have heard that name before.* She looked beautiful and somehow, familiar. He tried to shrug it off, but it nagged at him in the back of his mind. *No matter,* he thought to himself. He resolved to find her at the university. He had never noticed her in any of his classes. How could he have been so stupid? He wanted to know more about her. He wanted to talk with her. He fantasized about talking with her about everything, for hours. There was so much he wanted to know about her. He was, as they say, love-struck.

That night he tossed and turned in his bed. He could not get her off his mind; her smile, her voice, the way she had looked at him and tended to his now very sore and bruised arm. He was finally dreaming. He was chasing his brother down the beach. They ran with a kite and it flew higher and higher into the sky. It was at the Ancón Beach. They ran faster and faster as the kite soared higher and higher. He was not looking where he was going, and suddenly hit someone. The dream went into slow motion as he fell headlong towards the sand, noticing as he fell that he had hit another person. It was a girl, with brown hair and bright, brown eyes that flashed fire at him as he skidded into the beach and she fell backwards, arms flailing in the air. Those eyes, they looked so familiar. There was a huge wave that came up quickly and washed over him. He was suddenly twisting and turning in the current and choking. He awoke with a start and sat upright in bed, sweating and gasping for air. The cool night breeze blew through his window, chilling him and making him shudder. His heart was beating very fast. He remembered the eyes of the girl, and then a lightning strike hit him. That girl from so long ago on the beach in Ancón! Her name was *Emelia*! Could it be possible? The memory flooded back to him; the kite, the girls laughing, and his desperate search for her. My God, how long ago had that been...twenty years ago? Now to find her here, at the same university he attended? What were the odds of that? His mind whirled with so many thoughts. It was hard to imagine that it was even possible. He glanced at his old alarm clock. It was 5:48 in the morning. He threw off his covers and headed to the small kitchen to make some tea. There would be no more sleep tonight. He had never so looked forward to going to class in his life. He would get to university early today and begin his search.

Emelia had not slept well either. It was not due to thinking about Bernardo, but because her crazy neighbors had been up all night partying and playing loud music. She did not mind so much because they played popular rock and roll music; the Beatles, Led Zeppelin, and the Beach Boys. She had no idea what they were singing, but loved the music. She had memorized "I Want to Hold Your Hand" in English, and was able to impress her friend Rosario by knowing all the English lyrics. Even Rosario knew the chorus, and they would often sing loudly, "I wanna hold your hand!!!!" and laugh as the other students would stare at them. Still, she was irritated that the party had gone on until practically four o'clock in the morning. Didn't these crazy boys ever get any sleep? It was getting close to the end of the school year, and she would need to study for examinations. Clearly studying at home would not work. She thought about securing a place in the library, away from everyone, if possible.

She rose early, got ready for school and hopped on her Vespa, then headed towards the university. The scooter was the one indulgence she'd allowed her parents to spoil her with. All her friends had bicycles. She hated to admit it, and never would, especially to her Socialist friends, but she loved the little motorcycle. It was quick and light, allowing her to dart in and out of traffic efficiently, and the added bonus was she could leave her home later than on a bicycle and get to school more quickly. Sometimes she used it to go into the countryside, but she rarely went without a friend. It was too tempting a target for a thief, although most of the *compatriotas* that she knew in the surrounding villages also let everyone else know that she was not to be molested in any way. These kinds of sanctions and warnings came with swift reprisals if they were not obeyed. Just the same, Emelia was careful, and never stayed out past dark.

She breezed through the narrow streets of Cuzco until she reached the university. She parked close to the bicycle stands and removed the key, turning the front wheel to the right and locking it in place. Her first class was history. She wondered if she would see that boy again; what was his name? Oh yes, Bernardo. She walked into the crowded classroom and sat down. Seats were not assigned in the university, but she always chose to sit up close to the front. She liked to take scrupulous notes and listen closely to the professor. As was often the case, the professor rushed into the room, late as usual, followed closely by Bernardo, who was wildly scanning the room.

They locked eyes as the professor began saying in a loud voice, "All right, ladies and gentlemen, let's settle down, be seated, and let me mesmerize you once again with the history of the Mesoamerican civilizations…" There was some polite laughter and the clatter of chairs and desks being arranged, books being opened, and pens at the ready. Bernardo could only find a seat near the back, far away from Emelia. He waved at her slightly as he moved towards the back. She smiled at him briefly, and then focused her attention on the professor.

The class, which was normally an hour and a half long, seemed to take all day to Bernardo. Finally, it was 10:30, and the professor dismissed the class with a warning about final examinations coming in a month. Emelia got her things together into a wool bag she had bought from the local market, and headed for the door. Bernardo shoved his way past several students and caught up with Emelia as she was exiting the building.

"Hello!" he said to her, trying hard not to show he was out of breath. Emelia turned to him and smiled, pretending she barely knew who he was.

"Oh, hello, er, uh, Bernardo, wasn't it?" she smiled.

"Yes, yes, that's right," stammered Bernardo.

"How is that arm today? You had a nasty cut on it. Let me see it, is it better?" She reached for his sore arm. He winced as she touched the bruise on his elbow, and he pulled back.

"Oh, it's fine, much better." As she looked at him quizzically he confirmed, "No, really, it is!" He smiled back. "Listen, I had a wild dream last night, and I must ask you about something, do you mind?" He looked at her.

"What? What kind of dream?" said Emilia, wondering if this was some sort of come-on line.

"Well, it took place in a little seaside town north of Lima, perhaps you've heard of it, Ancón?"

"Why yes, I have. In fact, my family used to go there when we were small children; that is, until my grandmother died. We never went back after that. We were all too sad." Emelia

137

looked at the ground, suddenly thinking of her nana, and being filled with great sadness all over again.

"I'm sorry to hear that," said Bernardo.

"What about the dream?" she asked, pulling back from the distant sadness.

"Do you remember being on the beach with your sisters playing with a kite?" he asked, looking searchingly at her face.

"How do you know I have sisters? What's this all about?" She began to get alarmed, and yet she did remember something. A boy, helping her with her kite on the beach. He fixed the tail. It was the same day her grandmother had died! Suddenly, it came back to her in a flood; the boy, the kite, the ripping of his towel...

"Señor Ingeniero!" she said, amazed, as she put her hand up to her lips. "Oh, my God, it was *you* there that day!" Bernardo was nodding his head and smiling from ear to ear.

He said, "Can you imagine, after all this time, that we would meet again by chance in another place, hundreds of kilometers from where we first met? What are the chances of that happening?"

She smiled at him. She remembered him; there was a resemblance. She remembered the feeling of her first crush, and it made her warm inside. It was remarkable! *Bernardo,* she thought. Yes, that *was* his name. She grabbed his hands and jumped up and down.

"This is so cool!" she said.

"Can we go and talk for a while?" Bernardo asked, and they both suddenly became aware that they were holding each other's hands.

"Why not?" she said. "Where?"

"I don't know; how about the quadrangle?" suggested Bernardo. The quadrangle was a large, open area of grass surrounded by the university buildings, where all manner of students sat and studied, threw Frisbees, talked, debated, and occasionally would kiss secretly behind trees. They picked up their belongings off the sidewalk and walked towards the grassy area without saying a word. Bernardo picked a spot far enough from any group of people so that they could have privacy. He was so elated he could hardly speak.

They sat down on Bernardo's jacket and began to talk. They talked way past all of their classes, well into the late afternoon, when they suddenly became aware of the clanging of the bells of the tower announcing 5:00 p.m. "Oh, my gosh, it's so late. I totally forgot about my classes," she said to Bernardo. But for the first time in her university career, she didn't care at all. She was fascinated with Bernardo, and all the things he had told her about his family and plans for the future. She wanted him desperately to ask her out, but would never think of saying anything to him.

Bernardo said, "I guess we need to get back to our studies," absentmindedly getting to his feet and helping her up.

"Yes," she said, looking into his eyes.

He started to say, "Would you like to go out for dinner toni—?"

"Yes, yes I would!" she said, without even letting him finish his sentence. The both laughed. It had been such a wonderful day. It couldn't just end with going home, not now. And so, they ate for the first of many times at the Café Ayllu on the Plaza de Armes, and continued their conversation until closing time. From that day on, they were nearly inseparable.

Emelia was studying a relatively new type of science: biochemistry, or more specifically, phytochemistry, which is devoted to the biology of plants. It involved the study of the chemical aspects of plant life processes, including the chemical products of plants. Many international companies, especially the Americans, were very interested in many of the plants that lived only in South America, for use in the development of medicine and other products. Her professors had encouraged her, even though she was a woman, to pursue this as a career. So study she did, and as she talked to Bernardo about botany, and genetics, and chromatography, she could see his attention begin to wander. But he listened to her chatter on about herbs and ancient herbal medicine and phytochemicals, and studied her beautiful face. He would listen to her for hours, and occasionally try to ask something intelligent. She was impressed that he even bothered to listen. She had stacks of notebooks on every imaginable subject in her field, all carefully organized and titled. Everything in them was handwritten and underlined in different colored pencils. He supposed there was some meaning to the colors, but never asked. All he saw were pages upon pages of carefully handwritten notes. Bernardo was impressed with her organization and determination. She would no doubt become a successful scientist someday, he was sure of that.

Chapter Twelve - The American

1974

Bob Parks was born and raised in New York in the late '40s, along with his fraternal twin brother. His parents, a mismatched pair of war veterans, were married in 1945, right at the end of WWII. It was an unusual romance between a scholarly poor boy from Long Island, and a wealthy aristocrat from Boston. He was an ex-Catholic (he always liked to say that), and she was from a very unorthodox Jewish family that, among other things, practiced Christmas. How on earth they found each other and fell in love, Bob had always wondered, especially during his teenage years when the family struggled with his dad's alcoholism and the ensuing, and ever-increasing, nightmare that became all their lives.

Dad graduated from Columbia University *cum laude*, and later became a teacher with the New York City school system. Mom became a housewife, raising her twin sons, and shielding them from the raging craziness that had become their marriage. It was a life of ups and downs; of short calm periods, followed by angry tirades and fights. The boys never knew what to expect when they came home from school. Life in those days was always anxiety-ridden and fearful.

Above all things, education and making a good living was the prized goal of all middle-class families in the United States during the '50s and '60s. It was expected that if you worked hard, and got a decent education, that life would be better for you and your children. The American Dream was a life script in Bob's world: graduate from high school, go to college, maybe get a master's degree, get a good job, meet a girl, settle down and get married, have kids, and buy a house. All that was humming along just fine with some minor ups and downs, when suddenly, in 1968, without any warning, Bob's life was radically changed. His brother was diagnosed with non-Hodgkin's lymphoma. At the time, there was no treatment to speak of, although the family did their best and tried, but it was essentially a death sentence. In a few short months, the cancer ravaged his young body, and he died at the age of 20, leaving behind a devastated family. His dad's drinking increased, his mother became more despondent and desperate. In the end, after 33 years of marriage, they divorced.

Bob went to college at Iowa State University in Ames, Iowa. The school was internationally known for its work with the hybridization of crops; genomics, and cytogenetics, especially corn and other key grains grown in the United States and exported to other countries. The university was well endowed with grants from its chief multinational corporate "sponsor," GMBI. In fact, many of the finest graduate students went on to have lifetime careers with GMBI and continue their post-graduate research.

So it was with Bob upon his graduation from the university in 1975. His master's degree helped him acquire a position in one of GMBI's research centers, in Kansas City, Missouri. This was where he met his sweetheart, Janet Atkinson, who had just graduated from Stephens College, an all-girls' school in the pristine little town of Columbia, Missouri. It was only 126 miles away from where Bob had landed his first "big" job. Stephens was a great "trolling" area for young, eligible bachelors. Janet was a young teacher, fresh out of school, teaching the seventh grade of the Eleanor Post Middle School. Most of the girls that attended Stephens College were from upper-middle-class homes, and marrying into a wealthy family was another advantage of falling in love with Janet, especially starting out as a young engineer in the little-known field called bio-engineering. He was paid well by GMBI, but worked long hours and had little time for friends or socializing if he wanted to climb the corporate ladder.

Research and development in the emerging "Agro Business," as it was being called, was a fascinating career. Since the 1974 development of an extremely effective herbicide called glyphosate, companies like GMBI had been experimenting with the notion that crops like corn, wheat, barley, rape weed (from which canola oil is made), flaxseed, and so on, could be genetically altered in such a way that spraying glyphosate on them would only kill the weeds, not the crop. This was the birth of Genetically Modified Organisms, or GMOs. At first blush, it seemed like a fantastic idea. Farmers got higher yields, and thus made more money. Companies like GMBI sold the herbicides in inexhaustible amounts, and they made money on the GMO seed they had spent years of research developing.

Bob stared at the envelope on his desk from Peru. The address was from an E. Podera, in some mysterious city called Cuzco. It had been sitting with a bunch of other mail on his desk for about a week. He had not had time to open it because of the long hours he had been putting in with GMBI. Janet was not happy with him. They hardly saw each other except when he got in or out of bed, grabbed a cup of coffee, and pecked her on the cheek while running out the door. He pulled his father's letter opener from his cup that held pens, pencils, and all manner of office supplies; scissors, mini-stapler, and so on. Slicing open the lightweight airmail paper, he opened the letter and began to read:

Dear Mr. Parks,

My name is Emelia Mercedes Sanchez Podera. I am currently enrolled in graduate school at the National University of San Antonio Abad, in Cuzco, Peru, working on my doctoral degree. I have been specializing my studies in phytochemistry for the past three years. I have read a number of your published works in the American Association for the Advancement of Science *journals, and was intrigued by your latest publication: "The Vicissitudes of Genetically Modified Organisms in Resolving World Hunger." I would be curious to know if you would be interested in opening an international dialogue on this subject, as my country, Peru, is in desperate need of developing solutions for our people. Poverty in our country is extremely high, and the prospect of bringing cheaper and higher-yield grains and vegetables could be life-changing for our country. I realize you are very busy with your research, but I also have some interesting studies of my own that I would like to share with you, should you be interested, which I feel could be mutually beneficial for each of us. I look forward to corresponding further with you. Thank you, Emelia M. S. Podera., BS, MS*

Bob put down the thin paper on his desk and thought to himself, *This could be a big perk for GMBI and for me.* He thought about how to proceed.

He rolled a clean sheet of paper into his IBM Selectric II typewriter. It was a wonder of modern technology, with its interchangeable "type balls." One could change fonts with a simple click of a lever, and it had correctable film ribbon which easily lifted off mistakes in typing, and allowed corrections to be made without the fuss of Wite-Out, a correction fluid that often left documents, and the writer's fingers, looking rather messy. He began to compose his response to Ms. Podera.

Dear Ms. Podera,

Thank you so much for your interest in my work. I'm flattered that anyone outside the United States has even heard of our work here at GMBI, and AAAS. It would be a great honor to collaborate on some work together. However, I will have to have a signed and notarized Non-Disclosure Agreement before our conversations proceed in earnest. If you would be kind enough to sign the attached NDA, have it notarized and returned to me at your earliest convenience, I would be very interested in comparing notes with you. (He thought

secretly to himself that her notes were probably worthless, but never leave a stone unturned…)
Thank you for your interest in GMBI. I look forward to speaking with you further.

Sincerely,
Robert A. Parks, PhD
Senior Fellow for Cytology Research

RAP/chd
Attachment: GMBI NDA

He rolled the remaining paper out of the typewriter and put it in his "Out" bin for his secretary, Cathy Donnelly, to pick up, and attach the proper documentation and send it back to Peru.

1989

By now, Bob and Emelia had become international colleagues in the ever-expanding field of GMOs. They regularly exchanged papers and research, with the full cooperation of GMBI. They had big plans for a new potential market: South America. Emelia was always given just enough information to continue the dialogue, but never what was fully going on behind the scenes. Bob always felt a little guilty about the deception, yet he was gaining valuable pieces of information from her own research that was, in turn, helping him with his.

Because the Peruvian press paid little or no attention to the United States' farming industry, it was not widely known that many American farmers were being sued by GMBI for patent infringement and/or breach of contract in connection with its genetically engineered seed. The farmers, the suits alleged, were holding back seed to plant the following year, as was typical for all farmers, or using seed from grain elevators for replanting. Unfortunately, many of the farmers had not read the fine print on their contracts with GMBI. Other farmers in the later '90s began discovering herbicide-resistant crops growing in their fields, crops that they never intentionally planted. Clearly, research showed by the legal defense that the GMBI plants' pollen, and perhaps the wind, birds, or some other harmless act of nature had spread seeds. Nevertheless, reasoned GMBI, the farmers were violating licensing terms and were subject to patent infringement and were sued, successfully.

Of course, GMBI had its own legal problems, ranging from illegal toxic chemical dumps around the United States, to introducing what many considered toxic substances into the food supply through artificial hormones in cows, and also milk and other dairy products, and on and on and on....

1999

Time and careers had moved on. Robert was now a Senior Research Fellow with GMBI, overseeing almost all work conducted in their GMO division. He and Janet had divorced in 1992, another corporate casualty of climbing the ladder and ignoring his wife and family for fame and fortune. He was lonely at times, but the job kept him busy, and he was making a lot of money. One day, Robert received a surprising e-mail from Emelia, which read as follows:

Hello Robert,

I recently attended a symposium in Lima and listened to, among other presenters, a group from your company, GMBI. There were two gentlemen in particular, a Sr. Hector Valenzuala, and Sr. Luis Castellano, who seemed to be very interested in speaking with me after the meetings. We discussed some of my research that had been shared by you with them, apparently, and I was a bit alarmed at the direction the conversation took when I commented on the lawsuits I have seen occurring in your country against American farmers. They told me that these were nothing for me to concern myself about, and because of ongoing litigation, they couldn't speak with me about it anyway.

They asked me a lot about my work; where I did it, and most peculiarly, about my husband Bernardo and what he did, where he went on his trips as an exporter, and so on. Do you know anything about this?

I feel as if there is something going on "behind the scenes" as you say. Please advise, Emelia

Robert did not like surprises or bad news. This seemed to be both. It looked as if Valenzuala and Castellano had jumped the gun, or more aptly, shot themselves in the foot. Parks had been collaborating with Emelia Podera for many, many years. The plan all along had been to steal her research to speed up the process of a genetically modified seed that could become sterile after one planting, thus eliminating greedy farmers, lawsuits, and an increase in profitability worldwide. This was not the plan; no, not at all. He would have to stall her, and try to keep the relationship alive without alarming her any further. He slammed his fist on the desk so hard that his beloved crystal "Employee of the Year" ear of corn bounced to the floor and broke into pieces.

"Damn it!" he shouted. Half the office turned in the direction of his glassed-in corner office, and then just as quickly, looked away again. Robert Parks was not a guy to mess with. He would need to personally oversee this operation more closely. They were so close! He picked up his telephone and dialed a long distance number in Lima, Peru.

"Hello, General? Parks here. We need to talk."

Chapter Thirteen - Bernardo

Present Day

Bernardo studied the blue thread he held in his hand carefully. He pulled a small notebook out of his jacket pocket and wrote down the type and location of several of the knots. Some were simple overhand knots; some were so-called long knots consisting of an overhand knot with one or more additional turns, and some, figure eight knots. Their placement and repetition was how he had decoded the latitudes and longitudes on this particular string. He finished his notations, picked up the torch, and left the vault. Getting the giant balancing rock to close looked difficult, if not impossible, since the round stone he had wedged in the groove was pretty securely weighted down. The Incas had thought of that, too. To the side of the long groove that the round stone lay in were crosswise grooves as well, allowing the round stone to be slid sideways, with the help of a little moss or mud, thus letting the giant balancing stone swing back upwards to close the door. Placing his entire body on the tilted end, after greasing the groove with a handful of moss, he pushed hard on the round stone and it rolled relatively easily into the side groove. As he pushed himself up and off the huge stone, it slowly began to pivot back towards the balancing point, and he heard the vault door slide shut. The degree of craftsmanship and engineering of the Incas never ceased to amaze him.

He headed back to the hacienda. It was already mid-morning, and he had not eaten. He was hungry, but the results of his little expedition and hypothesis needed to be checked. He looked around as he walked back along the paths towards his hacienda. He had been trained long ago to be constantly aware of his surroundings at all times. It had become a habit that had saved his life on any number of occasions, especially lately. No one was in sight except for a few of the local laborers working the fields. It was harvest time for many of the crops, so burros were being loaded with long stalks of corn and bags of potatoes to take to the market for sale. Life in the mountains was very simple, and had not changed much for hundreds of years. There was very little mechanization. Nearly all the farming was done on small family plots and all by hand, from plowing to planting to harvest. Bernardo headed up the last hill towards Nido de Búho. When he arrived, Maria smiled and suggested politely that his breakfast was still waiting for him. He smiled back, entered through the main doorway, and went straight to the dining room, where a spread of fresh bread, fresh juices, cheese, meat, and fruit awaited him. Maria brought out hot coca tea and poured him a cup, then left the room immediately. He ate quickly, not really thinking about the food.

His mind was on other things. He took a last sip of his tea and went upstairs to his room to retrieve his briefcase. He then went to the main living room and opened his briefcase, turning on his laptop, plugging in the power cord, and extracting the note with the knotted string attached from two days ago. He took the notebook out of his jacket and examined the drawings and knot configurations he had made back at the storehouse. His laptop came up, and he opened his Internet browser to check something very specific: the exact latitude and longitude of his apartment in Miraflores. Google Earth placed it at 12 °07'14.43'S by 77 °02'34.65W on Malecón Cisneros. He looked at his notes, and then at the string attached to the mysterious list.

The knots were tiny. He needed to use the magnifying glass that he always had next to him for fine print. He checked the knots. They were the same type of knots he had been looking at no more than an hour ago, only in miniature. He dug into his briefcase and pulled out an old folder. It was his research from many years ago. In his notes, he had compiled a table that translated knots to numbers and meanings. He wrote down the numbers, and scanned back and forth from string to knots to table and back again. To his shock, the numbers matched almost to the exact degree the longitude and latitude he had just gotten off the Internet. It was like saying through a quipu, "…and I also know where you live!" "What the hell?" said Bernardo out loud. He dropped all his papers on the floor. His hands began to shake as he bent over to pick up the papers that had scattered around his feet. Someone close to him had to be behind this. Very few people knew of his work, his findings, or his affiliation with Los Cóndores de Oro, except other members. *Was this some type of power play?* he wondered to himself. He found himself suddenly trusting no one. His mind raced…but who? Was it one person, or several persons?

His cell phone rang, startling him back to his living room. He looked at the caller ID, "Unknown wireless caller" was all the screen read.

"Hello?" said Bernardo.

"Señor Villacorta, this is Captain Sanchez of the Lima Police. I wanted to let you know we have found the shooter who attacked you at your apartment."

"Really?" said Bernardo, a bit surprised. Based on the odds that Victor had told him only a few nights earlier, he found that quite surprising.

"And who is this person?" he asked.

"Well, that's a bit of a problem; we're not sure, exactly."

Bernardo rolled his eyes up towards the ceiling and then said with polite impatience, "And that would be because..."

"Well, because he was dead when we found him, señor, with nothing on his body that would help us identify him. His throat had been slashed. The Serenazgo found him in an alley not far from your apartment. They called us."

"And how do you know this was the guy that was the shooter?" Bernardo interrupted, his patience waning.

"We found three items on his body. One was a piece of paper with your exact address on it, and two expended brass cartridges in his pocket. And," he continued, "the prints off the shell casings we showed you from the roof matched two of the prints from his right hand."

Bernardo thought, *out of how many sets of prints?* but said aloud, "But you have no idea who he is or where he came from?"

"No, señor," said the policeman.

"Captain, you said there were three items you found, but you only mentioned two; the paper with my address and the shell casings. Was there something you left out?"

"Oh, yes, but I thought it was of no consequence."

"Let me be the judge of that, Captain; what was it?"

"A few grains of quinoa," said the captain.

"Quinoa?" said Bernardo, and felt a slight shudder go through him. "Any lab analysis on it?" he asked cautiously.

"Yes. One of our lab students recognized it as a GMO; you know, he called them genetically modified organisms? I guess he might have been a farmer or something, I really don't know. It didn't seem relevant to this investigation. Does this have any meaning to you, señor?" he asked.

"Ah, no, no, I don't think so." He thought about what it might mean. There was a silence of a few seconds.

"Hello?" said the captain.

"Ah, yes, I'm still here," said Bernardo. "Have you checked his prints against any police databases you have?" Now Bernardo really wanted to know who this dead man was.

"Yes, señor, we're working on it now. Also we're checking with the United States CIA and INTERPOL as well."

"Very well, Captain, please let me know more when and if you find out anything else about this guy."

"Si, señor, I will."

"Thank you for your call, Captain," Bernardo said, and abruptly hung up.

More questions with no answers. Who was this guy? Was he killed because he failed his mission, or just because he was expendable? Where did they get all this information? His suspicion that there was a leak somewhere from within was growing steadily. No one could know the kinds of things that were being made known to him except someone who already knew them. He needed to look up one of his sources in Cuzco. He thought it best, under the circumstances lately, to not use his driver, Juan, but to just go by himself.

He grabbed the keys off the front table, jumped into the car, and headed for Cuzco. He drove probably faster than he should have, winding left and right, up and down, and always mindful that around every bend could be anything from a huge truck to a herd of goats crossing the road. Today, the road was clear all the way to Cuzco. He weaved in and out of traffic, heading for the Plazoleta de Las Nazarenas. Just off the tiny plaza on Purgatorio (he loved the irony) was a tiny apartment. The person he was looking for was nearly always there, so he had not bothered to call. He was also wondering whether his cell phone calls were being triangulated, so better to just show up.

He parked the car and walked into the small open area of the building. He knocked on a plain, but pretty blue door. A moment later, a woman answered from behind the door.

"Si? Who is it?"

"Bernardo, señora, please let me in."

"Bernardo? Oh, my God! Wait, just a moment, please!"

He heard footsteps scurrying away from the door, a pause, and then hurrying back. The door flew open. "Bernardo! How wonderful to see you!" She hugged him and pushed him back, holding onto his arms to stare into his eyes.

"What a pleasant surprise. What brings you here? Why didn't you call first? My place is such a mess."

"Anna, please don't worry about your home, it's always spotless." He laughed, and gestured to the open door. "May I come in?"

"Oh, yes, please. I'm sorry. Where are my manners?" She led him into the apartment, closing the door behind them, and padded barefoot down the narrow hallway to a small but comfortably decorated living room. Bernardo sat down and studied his sister-in-law. She was Emelia's second-youngest sister, and just as beautiful in her fifties as she had been when he and Emelia had married so long ago. They had talked briefly at Emelia's funeral a few weeks earlier, but there were so many people, and somehow they never connected for very long. He wanted to speak with her about several matters.

"Can I get you some tea, or something to eat, or both?" Anna smiled at him. She had always admired her brother-in-law from afar.

"Tea would be nice; thanks, Anna."

She got up to head for the kitchen. "All right if I use your bathroom?" he yelled down the narrow hallway towards the kitchen.

"Sure. There are clean towels in the small closet to the right!"

He went into the tiny bathroom and scanned the room as he urinated. Next to the closet was a small antique stand of drawers, with photographs on the top, and a variety of jewelry scattered about. He finished and washed his hands, reaching for a towel from the closet. He saw four tiny drawers at the top of the stand. Out of curiosity, and bad habit, he opened each drawer and quickly scanned its contents. Mostly earrings, and various pins and broaches in two of the drawers. One held nothing but rings. The last drawer held some faded black and white photographs and a gold necklace. He began to shut the drawer when he heard a clatter against the side of the drawer holding the pictures. He pulled it open quickly. Sliding to the front of the drawer was a small golden condor pin. He studied it for a moment. It was old and slightly corroded. He was only too familiar with what it was, and what it represented. He put it back in the drawer and slid the drawer shut quickly. His head was spinning. Anna? She's in this, too?

"Everything all right? Did you find the towels, Bernardo?" Anna yelled down the hallway.

"Er, yes. I'll be right out!"

"Well hurry, or your tea will be cold!"

Bernardo quickly wiped off his hands and made his way back to the living room. He sat on the comfortable couch, moving pillows out of the way. What was it with women and pillows? They served no purpose, but they were always on all manner of furniture, couches, beds…. Anna had set out her best tea set with some small alfajores on a plate. She poured him some tea, no doubt Mate de Coca, and handed him the tea and the plate of cookies. "Alfajores?"

"Well, all right. Perhaps just one, especially since I know you made them." Bernardo knew she would never buy this delicacy. His hands were visibly shaking when he held both the teacup and the cookie. She didn't seem to notice.

"So, Bernardo, you never answered my question. What brings you here today?" She smiled at him as if she were hoping it was for no reason other than to see her. She had always had a fondness for her brother-in-law, and now that her sister had passed away, well…her brother-in-law was always friendly, but all business.

"I wanted to ask you a question about Emelia, and I also have something for you that I know she wanted you to have. Did you ever talk with Emelia about my research on the quipus?"

"No," she said, sipping her tea. "We did talk about your studies of Incas in general, and the work you were doing for the mining company back in the '70s, but never about quipus. Why?"

He studied her face carefully, looking for any sign of deception. While her face showed some expression of questioning, it did not seem sincere somehow. Also, he noticed that she pushed her hair back away from her eyes while she was responding to him. She was lying.

"I found a piece of paper back in Lima with a string tied to it with knots on it. The next day someone tried to kill me—a sniper."

"What?" Her hand flew up to her mouth. "Oh my God, Bernardo! Were you hurt? Why would someone want to kill you?"

"A good question; unfortunately, one I don't have the answer to. But no, he missed. Twice."

"Does this have anything to do with quipus?" Anna was wasting no time cutting to the chase.

"Not sure. It's still a little mysterious. I felt coming up here was safer after the last few days of excitement. The police found the shooter in Lima; in fact, I just got a call from the chief of police before I left to come here."

"Was it someone you knew?" Anna asked, leaning into the conversation slightly. He thought that was an odd question, but kept the thought to himself.

"No, and it will be hard to find out who he was. They found him dead in an alley near my flat in Miraflores."

"My God, this is so frightening. Have you spoken to Victor about all this?"

He tried not to register any reaction. How the hell would she know about Victor? As far as he knew, they had never even met.

"Victor? Who is Victor?" He played stupid.

"Why, General Victor de la Hoya, of course. Bernardo, I know you and Emelia were friends of his for many years; she told me you were close friends and worked together in business matters. Naturally I thought of him because of his position in the military, and that he would be of help to you now with this horrible incident." She smiled slightly. "You look surprised, Bernardo. I know a lot of things about my favorite brother-in-law. Perhaps more than you want me to." She laughed and looked into his eyes. *I guess you do,* Bernardo thought to himself.

"I also had contact with Victor over the years when I was with the Department of Agriculture. He was always very helpful, especially when we were working with the Americans in the '80s and had to be protected from the Shining Path." Anna had graduated at the head of her class in university, just like her older sister, receiving top honors in bioengineering, at the time a fledgling science in South America. She had gotten top offers from many American companies who wanted her assistance in introducing genetically modified hybrids to her native country, a country that thrived on corn; 55 varieties of corn. The plan had not worked out, the Americans withdrew, and Anna was left with a small job in a small Argentinean-based company doing research for them.

"Well, I guess I had always thought, ahh, well, that is…" he stammered, giving himself away. "I was surprised, honestly, that you knew the general, but yes, I have spoken with him about all of this. He's trying to help. What I came here to ask you was about GMOs. Have any of those Americans you had dealings with in the '80s tried to contact you in the last few months?"

"You must be pretty freaked out by all of this," she said, changing the subject abruptly as she rose from her chair and moved over to sit next to him on the couch. *Very* close to him on the couch. Bernardo found himself both stimulated and uncomfortable. Anna's perfume was light but very feminine, and somehow soothing. Something he had not felt in quite some time began to stir in his gut. Anna folded her legs, revealing a very attractive thigh through the slit in her skirt. *Mierda!* he thought to himself. *My sister-in-law is seducing me!* He attempted to move away towards the end of the couch and speak, but before he could open his mouth, her hand was on his knee.

"Where are you going, Bernardo? Are you afraid of me?" she smiled.

"Ahhh, no, not exactly. But, Anna, what is going on here? I mean, I feel very uncomfortable. What about the question I asked you?" He felt the blood rising in his neck. My God, he was blushing. Anna was genuinely enjoying his discomfort.

"The answer to your question is no. You know I have always found you very attractive, Bernardo. And now with Emilia gone, I thought you must still have, you know, needs?" She barely whispered the last part of the sentence.

"What?" Bernardo asked in fumbling discomfort. He felt like a schoolboy. Emelia was the only woman he had been intimate with for more than thirty years, and yet, he felt himself getting an erection. He stood up suddenly and looked at Anna, trying to look angry, but not being able to pull it off, especially with the obvious tent in his pants. "I think I'd better go now," he announced, as he started to move towards the door.

"But, Bernardo, I meant no harm. Surely you don't need to leave so soon. We were just starting to get to the interesting part!" She laughed as she stood up and came towards him. She reached out to give him a hug, throwing her arms around his neck and pressing her body against him. "Hmmm," she quipped, "another part of your body doesn't seem to want to leave." She reached down and stroked his erection. "If talking about GMOs does this for you, we can talk more… at least for a while."

"Anna, I'm flattered, really," he said, as he pushed her back from him and held her at arm's length. "I just don't think this is a good idea. I need to go." That was what his mouth said, but his mind was already chasing her down the hallway into her bedroom and having hot, passionate sex with her. He needed to go now, or that was exactly what was going to happen. Anna laughed and leaned forward to kiss him.

"All right, Bernardo. But don't come back here again unless you expect to stay a lot longer. You and I have unfinished business!" she purred, and she laughed again. She was as beautiful as her sister, he thought to himself. He headed for the door.

"Oh!" he said, as he fumbled in his pants pocket. He extracted the small box he had been carrying and handed it to Anna.

"What is this?" She reached out to accept the box, her fingers lingering on his hand for a moment.

"I know Emelia would want you to have it. Open it." She opened the box to reveal an enormous ruby encased in an ornate gold ring. It was the ring he had given Emelia for their anniversary, when he had first discovered the Inca storehouse not far from where they were now.

"Oh!" Her eyes grew wide and she slipped the ring on her finger, holding her hand out to examine it. "It's beautiful, Bernardo. It's magnificent! Thank you. I'm not sure I could ever wear this anywhere without fear of losing it to a thief; or losing my finger *and* the ring," she laughed. "But this is so sweet of you, and so generous." He reached for the door before she could hug him again. He knew if she did, he'd never leave.

"You're welcome, Anna, and now I have to leave." He opened the front door and practically ran for the street.

"Good-bye, Bernardo!" Anna shouted to his back. "Please be careful….and do come back!"

Bernardo didn't look back. He walked swiftly to where he had left his car. *Damn it!* he thought to himself. *She's good. I never would have expected that move, and she knew it!* Clearly he had underestimated his sister-in-law's ability to manipulate and steer him away from what he had come to find out. He felt like a fool. He also felt a pull to return and indulge himself in suppressed desire, which he thought was always the most passionate and exciting. That would have to wait. He started his car, and headed towards the country.

CHAPTER FOURTEEN

By the time he returned to Nido de Búho it was early evening, and there was a chill starting to descend from the mountains. As he entered the hacienda, he noticed a package sitting on the front table, along with some mail. It would normally have been impossible to receive mail and packages so far out in the country, but many years ago, applying several hundred soles to the district official in charge of the post office assured that any mail would arrive promptly at this home.

Maria appeared from the kitchen, inquiring about supper. He said soup, cheese, and a bit of fresh bread would be sufficient. He wasn't very hungry. He picked up the package from the table and examined it. It was postmarked from Toquepala, in southeastern Peru. He shook the box, which rattled slightly. He decided to open it up. He pulled the explosive sensor from his jacket and ran it around the entire box. All green, no evidence of a bomb. He used his knife to open the paper and tape that held it together. Inside the box, padded loosely with newspaper, were a few rocks, which he recognized as malachite, and some copper wire. He studied the malachite with its rich green and black colors. This was an ore sample from one of the mines in southern Peru.

He dug into the box and found a scribbled note on a piece of paper in pencil. It read, *repetir el 2006?* 2006 was the last time Los Cóndores de Oro made a "little adjustment" in the copper industry. When all was said and done, it really was all about supply and demand. Peru and Chile and a few other nations were in need of revenues. They made the request to a few discreet members, and the availability of copper suddenly became extremely scarce, with accompanying cover stories about mining disasters, high demand from the electric companies, etc. The price of copper shot through the roof. So high in fact, that reports were circulating lately that it was worthwhile, especially in the United States, to steal the copper tubing from air conditioning units for scrap. Before the "adjustment," copper was fetching less than $.75 cents per pound on the open market. Now it was selling for over $3.00 per pound. Problem solved.

He also found a small brown envelope at the bottom of the box. He took it out and poured the contents into the palm of his hand. There were about ten small round white seeds.

They appeared to be quinoa. He examined the envelope again. Stamped on the back was the number "34H31" and the name, he supposed, of a company, because it had a logo of a sprouting plant, GMBI, Inc.™. He sat down at his computer and googled GMBI, Inc. He got 239,256 hits. GMBI, as he read page after page of stories and on their home page, was Genetically Modified Biotech International, a huge multinational conglomerate that specialized in GMOs.

The more he read, the more he began to understand the meaning of the package, or at least he had a pretty good idea. Ninety percent of all the corn and assorted other grains in the United States were GMOs with a patent that belonged to GMBI. That meant two things: 1) They had monopolized that crop in the U.S. and had to be paid "royalties" because each seed used by the farmers was considered "intellectual property," and as such was protected by the United States Patent Office; and 2) It was a self-perpetuating source of revenue due to the fact that the seeds had been genetically altered to only be used once, meaning they were sterile, and the seeds produced by the plant could not be used to re-plant the following year. It was a whole new area of wealth and power that he had never even considered. Ultimately, when you followed the argument to its most ridiculous consideration, it meant simply that this company ultimately controlled *food*! The concept hit him like a punch in the gut.

Who needs weapons of mass destruction? You control food, you control the people. Never have to fire a single shot. It was utterly amazing in its simplicity, and the strategy was undeniably brilliant. His mind spun with the possibilities. He queried Google further. What about South America? What was happening here in his own hemisphere?

Much was happening in Paraguay, apparently. GMBI had all but taken over the soybean market in the country. Agribusiness was alive and well. The small local farmers were being pushed out or driven out one by one. They were replaced with enormous fields of soybeans. The forests were being cleared at an alarming rate and, as might be expected, the entire ecosystem was being swallowed up by an industry that had an insatiable appetite for land and control. Clearly, the entire Paraguay government had been bought and paid for. The Minister of Agriculture was driving a new Mercedes and had several homes, even one in Peru. Now flooding and contaminated water supplies were beginning to make the news.

Stories of cancer clusters that had never before been seen in the country were increasing geometrically every few years. And the farmers, who had ransomed their very lives to get rich, were now owned by GMBI; indirectly, of course. They had to purchase new seeds every year, and immense equipment to till and harvest their crops. These were machines and seeds they could not afford, but through generous donations by GMBI to the people of Paraguay, the Minister of Agriculture made the machines and seeds available as loans against the crops the farmers were growing. They had become, in fact, indentured servants to the state. GMBI paid handsome royalties to the country, none of which ever made it below cabinet level, but nevertheless bought any new law or statute needed to assure successful business "partnerships" with the country. Ironically, the few farmers that remained were poorer than they had ever been when they had their own tiny farms. Now they had no animals (they took up vital growing lands) to feed themselves, no money, and food now had to be bought from stores. These company stores were conveniently located in the tiny farm communities, and offered all manner of exotic and expensive meats, vegetables, fruits, and packaged goods. To survive, the family had to spend what little money they made from their crops to buy food to survive. Most perished in the first few years. Those that survived sent their families to the cities to find work.

So, in a way, and certainly under different circumstances, the story of wealthy landowners controlling and exploiting the poor and owning the land had come full circle with agribusiness. This was a situation rich with the potential for revolution, as it had been in the sixties and seventies with the Shining Path. Bernardo sighed, and closed the cover of his laptop. *Nothing really changes, just the players,* he thought to himself. So, what to do? He rolled the seeds around in the palm of his hand. Odd that this quinoa was the same thing the captain had found on the sniper's body that they had discussed yesterday. He needed to make a few more phone calls. The package, he now knew, was from Señor Gamarra. He "oversaw" eastern Peru, Northern Bolivia, and Western Brazil. There must be opportunities available. His first call would be to him.

But quinoa? This was an indigenous grain grown for centuries by the Incas in the Andes, and a sort of super-grain, or super-food. It was gluten-free and rich in iron, easy to digest, and high in protein. It was a perfect takeover for a cereal that was widely used all over South America. The potential for exploitation was not lost on him.

After finishing supper, he retrieved his satellite phone and dialed Angel Gamarra.

"Hello?" The voice on the phone was familiar and clear.

"Angel, buenas tardes, this is Bernardo calling." There was a momentary silence.

"Bernardo! I have to assume you're calling about the package I sent you. Did it arrive OK?" And then a bit hesitantly, "Is this line secure?"

"Yes, and yes, my friend. Don't concern yourself with such things. I can only think of two ways we should proceed with this package; forward, and embrace these food thieves, or against them. What's the plan?"

"We're thinking that a full meeting in our hacienda in Ica would be good. Say, next Thursday? Then we can feel more comfortable about these discussions, and also perhaps some of the events that have been occurring over the past few weeks. Are you all right?"

"Yes, although I have had some surprising meetings over the past day or so." Although the phone was ostensibly secure, they always talked in code anyway. Old habits die hard.

"I had an unfortunate 'accident' myself only yesterday. It involved a man and a woman in a car. They must have been drunk or something, tried to run me over. *In my own town!*" Angel could hardly contain the rage in his voice. So there were others besides himself and Montoya…

"I'm sorry to hear that, my friend. Are *you* all right?"

"Yes, but unfortunately, the two in the car, well, it did not go well for them. They ended up crashing into a tree and both were killed." There was a pause, and then a long sigh. "We should end this conversation, *cholo*. I'll see you in Ica next week, OK? Ciao." And then, abruptly, the line went dead.

For whatever reason, he wasn't sure, he felt that Angel's package was a bit coincidental, and also that a larger hand was at play here. Long ago he had learned to listen to that little voice in his head that suggested things. Some called it intuition. Was he being lured to Ica for another, more sinister purpose? He also thought of Emelia's notebooks from so long ago when they attended university together, and then her notes that continued into her career and research.

They were still in the library, carefully organized on three shelves, and dutifully dusted by the housekeeper once a week. Most were old and fading black and white composition tablets, but he remembered a conversation he and Emelia had had a few years before. She had retired from the Ministry many years ago, but he remembered her speaking of GMOs, and the concern that the Peruvian government was expressing to the Ministry. Perhaps there might be some "breadcrumb trail" he could follow in her notes.

It was an easier search than he had thought. The books were organized by year. He'd search through the latest notebooks, starting with the last few, and would work backwards.

He didn't need to look very far. He opened the last book and paged through the notes. The first few pages read more like minutes of the proceedings at the Ministry of Agriculture than they did about her own research; who was present, what areas of the Peruvian government they oversaw, and a number of company officials, of special note GMBI executives. Two: Sr. Hector Valenzuala, and Sr. Luis Castellano. Sr. Valenzuala apparently represented the research and development branch of the GMBI Genetics and Hybridization Group (GHG), and Sr. Castellano was the executive for that division. The notes went on in Emelia's neat handwriting to describe the various officials. There were little drawings and sketches on the sides of the pages, mostly of plants. It must have been a boring meeting. He thumbed through the pages of the last notebook, which was barely half-full of notes and writing. As he neared the middle, he noticed one of the pages seemed to have been cut out very carefully, probably with a sharp knife. It was close enough to the binding that it went almost unnoticed. The page after the cut had a slight cut from the knife that had deftly removed the page before.

The page before the cut-out page contained complicated equations, chemical symbols, and diagrams, which made no sense to Bernardo at all. There were little scribbled notes next to some of the equations, mostly scientific in nature, and using terms he did not understand, like "gene targeting" and "homologous recombination." The last one had tiny question marks neatly spaced around it. Below the equations was a very detailed picture,

	No mutation	**Point mutations**			
		Silent	**Nonsense**	**Missense**	
				conservative	non-conservative
DNA level	TTC	TTT	ATC	TCC	TGC
mRNA level	AAG	AAA	UAG	AGG	ACG
protein level	**Lys**	**Lys**	**STOP**	**Arg**	**Thr**

basic
polar

By Jonsta247 (Own work) [GFDL (http://www.gnu.org/copyleft/fdl.html) or CC BY-SA 4.0-3.0-2.5-2.0-1.0 (http://creativecommons.org/licenses/by-sa/4.0-3.0-2.5-2.0-1.0)], via Wikimedia Commons

These notes were clearly leading to the next page that was missing, but he sensed that Emelia was concerned about something. Her notes read, "By altering just one amino acid, the entire peptide may change, thereby changing the entire protein. If the protein functions in cellular reproduction, then this single-point mutation can change the entire process of cellular reproduction for this organism." It went on, "If the mutation occurs in the region of the gene where transcriptional machinery binds to the protein, the mutation can affect the binding of the transcription factors because the short nucleotide sequences recognized by the transcription factors will be altered. Mutations in this region can affect rate of efficiency of gene transcription, which in turn can alter levels of mRNA, and thus protein levels in general." That was the end of the page, then the missing page, and then the last page, which spoke about "consequences of the experiment" and notes to call various people whose names he didn't recognize, except for one: Miguel Montoya. *What the hell?* he thought to himself. It had only been a few short days ago that he was discussing Miguel's murder with Victor. Why would Emelia want to call him?

He sat down in the big chair in the library and collapsed into its softness with a sigh, marking the place in the notebook with his finger and closing it. His head was spinning. This had been a busy day. He tried to analyze what he was discovering. Montoya! What was his connection to all this? Was he dead because of it? When this had been written, he was just an aspiring political foot soldier in the APRA. Bernardo went over the details of that night with General Victor. Something nagged at his memory, of that piece of paper found on Montoya's body with the threat. There were numbers, or letters, or combinations of letters and numbers. They didn't make any sense at the time. He went back out to the hallway where he had opened the box. The envelope. There were numbers and letters stamped on it, "34H31." He grabbed the secure telephone and dialed the Ministry of Defense in Lima. Seconds passed. He glanced at his watch. It was already 11:45 in the evening. The phone rang and rang. *Come on,* he thought. *Pick up!*

Finally, the phone was answered. "Ministry of Defense, Sergeant Velasquez. How may I direct your call?"

"Ah, yes," Bernardo stammered out. His mind was racing. "This is Señor Bernardo Villacorta. I need to speak with General Victor de la Hoya immediately. It's a matter of great importance!" he nearly shouted into the phone.

"I'm sorry, Señor Villacorta, but the general has retired for the night. Perhaps you could try to reach him in the morning, he's—"

Bernardo cut him off before he could finish his sentence. He fought for control of his temper and tone of voice. "Sergeant, what was your name, Velasquez?"

"Yes, sir," the sergeant responded crisply.

"I'm a close, personal friend of the general. I know for a fact that if I have to tell him that you were unable to put this *very important call* through to him," he said through clenched teeth, "that you may find yourself in another line of work, like cleaning the shit out of toilets for the rest of your short career in the army! Now get me the general immediately! This is very important! Are we clear, Sergeant?"

The sergeant hesitated, clearly considering his options, and wondering which would be worse; waking the general and incurring his well-known wrath, or perhaps worse, cleaning latrines for the rest of his army stint. He didn't have to think long.

"Well?" Bernardo questioned, growing more and more impatient with each passing second.

"Yes, señor, I'll put your call through. I apologize for the delay, it's just that—"

Again Bernardo cut him off. "Now!" he spat into the telephone. The line went silent for a second, clicked, and then rang again. It rang and rang and rang. No one, it seemed, was going to pick up. "Damn Victor!" he thought as the phone droned on. "Probably either too much wine, a woman, or both."

The line clicked open. A sleepy General de la Hoya answered. "Yes? Who is this? Do you know what bloody time it is?" he yawned into the phone.

"Victor, it's me, Bernardo."

"Bernardo? I thought you were in Cuzco. What is it, my friend?"

He was clearing up. Victor knew there was no other reason for his friend to call this late unless it was important. He began worrying immediately. "Victor, I'm sorry to disturb you so late. I need to check something with you."

"Yes, of course, my friend. What is it?" The tone in his voice feigned deep concern.

"You remember that piece of paper that was found on Miguel's body that night of the murder?"

"Yes, yes I do. Why?"

"There were some numbers and letter combinations scribbled on it. Do you remember what they were? I know this is a weird request, but I think I've found something." Bernardo waited for a response. He heard a long sigh.

"Bernardo, I don't carry around evidence with me, and my memory is not quite what it used to be…" He chuckled to himself. "But I can try to find out for you. Do you need it right now? Everything is closed; it's late at night, for God's sake! What the hell do you need those numbers for?" He was starting to sound a bit impatient, and perhaps a bit anxious. Bernardo considered his next words carefully.

"It's a long story, Victor, and I won't bother you with the details right now, but I think I've discovered a possible connection in this case through some notes I've been reading in one of Emelia's notebooks, and a package I received today."

"Bernardo, I promise you, since this is so important, that I can get this information for you tomorrow and call you with it. I'll have to go to the National Police Headquarters and throw my weight around to get into the evidence room. They're handling this matter now, not the Ministry." Victor sounded as if he would be very happy to go back to sleep. Actually he would be making a number of phone calls himself as soon as he hung up with Bernardo.

"But, Victor," Bernardo began to sound anxious, "I *really* need to know that before tomorrow. I'm heading to Ica next week. This information could be helpful, very helpful."

"Ica?" the general asked. "What are you doing in Ica?"

Bernardo was growing impatient. Surely the general knew about the meeting. After all, Angel Gamarra was no stranger to the general. "Victor, there's a meeting of Los Cóndores de Oro; don't you know about it?" Bernardo was puzzled.

"Oh, ah, yes, I must have forgotten; there are so many meetings..." his voice trailed off for a moment. "Who told you about this...meeting?" The general was suddenly wide awake. Bernardo became more suspicious of the conversation. The general was anything but forgetful. Something was wrong.

"Angel," Bernardo answered. "We spoke on the phone this evening. He said it was very important. About, (he edited his conversation) some company. A multinational. That it was going to be a big deal."

There was silence on the other end of the line. "Victor?" Silence. "Victor? Are you there?"

"Yes, yes I'm here. I'm thinking. Bernardo, don't go to that meeting next week. Invent a reason. You're sick; you ate some bad food, something. I need to make some calls. Tell me you that you're not going to go until you hear from me tomorrow, all right?" His voice had a tone of both mild concern and authority.

"But—" He was cut off before he could finish.

"Damn it, Bernardo! Listen to me, and do what I tell you. Are you talking about GMBI? Something here is not right. Why are you being evasive? Is there someone else in the room listening to this conversation that you're not telling me about?" Paranoia was not one of Victor's normal moods. How did he know he was talking about GMBI??

"No, of course not, Victor," he stammered back. His mind was racing faster than he could respond to the conversation, which seemed to be taking a dangerous turn.

"Bernardo, there are forces at work here that you do not understand yet. Do not go to that meeting. Understand?" The general was adamant.

"Well, of course, Victor, if you think there's something up. I won't go. I'll stay here and make up a story, as you suggested. But get back to me tomorrow, please. And I need that letter thing, too."

"All right, my friend, good. I'll speak with you in the morning. Bernardo, be careful for right now. Do you have a weapon with you?"

"Yes, my Beretta."

"Start carrying it with you. For your own safety. It could be nothing, but one can't be too careful."

"All right, I will." Bernardo was now more concerned than when he had started connecting the dots tonight. "So, I'll speak with you tomorrow, Victor?"

"Yes. I'll try to contact you no later than noon tomorrow. Until then, don't go out too far from the house, all right? I'm going to be sending someone from a unit we have nearby to keep an eye on things."

"Is that really necessary, Victor? You're getting a little dramatic, aren't you?"

"Can't be too careful, my friend. Just feed them and make friends. I'll call you in the morning. Good night," and the line went dead.

The general was furious. All his efforts to keep Bernardo from being exposed to the meeting in Ica had failed. Angel certainly would be held accountable for this. He paced back and forth in his office. What if he finds the damned seeds that Emelia was working on? What if he finds out about any of this crap? He was going to have to handle this personally. There was no other choice.

His mind drifted back to the night they had killed Emelia. What a shame, she was so lovely. And Bernardo, it would be an equal shame to eliminate him, too, but there was too much as stake. First Bernardo, then Ica. He picked up his phone and made a few calls, one in particular to the United States.

CHAPTER FIFTEEN

Emelia had to suddenly go to Lima for the day and had returned later in the evening. She didn't say much more than she had to see a friend about some old project they had collaborated on quite a few years ago.

"I won't be long, darling," she had said, and took a fast car to the city. Oddly, he noticed she chose to drive herself instead of using one of the staff. A woman's prerogative. He had learned from many years of marriage when to question or interfere, and when to keep his mouth shut.

True to her word, she returned later that evening. They had a wonderful evening meal in their home in Ancón, and went for an after-supper walk along the swirling black and white terrazzo beachfront, as was their tradition when they stayed at the house. This place, the smells, the ocean, the fishing boats, were so familiar to both of them. After all, they had spent a good deal of their childhoods in this very special seaport. It had only seemed logical when Bernardo had become wealthy to return to this place of wonderful and sad memories. They held hands and chatted about the early summer this year, and how surprisingly chilly it was getting now that autumn was descending on Peru. Emelia was swatting away a few mosquitos as they walked. She slapped at a sharp bite at the nape of her neck. Without any warning, Emelia stopped abruptly, her eyes rolling backwards, and collapsed onto the cold terrazzo. She choked out a breathless cry to her husband, "Bernardo!"

"Emelia, my God! What's wrong?" He was totally taken off guard. One moment they were mindlessly strolling along as lovers do, and the next she was collapsed like a lifeless doll on the walkway. He stared for a moment at the pain in his wife's eyes, which were beginning to roll backwards, and realized something terrible was happening. He screamed for help as he knelt beside her. "Help! Help! Please! Someone call an ambulance! A doctor! Is there a doctor anywhere?" The boulevard was all but deserted. He glanced up, desperately scanning the apartments lining the seaside. Lights were coming on, windows were opening, and faces appeared, staring down at them. A lone figure with a long stick in his hands ran in the opposite direction and disappeared into the darkness.

"Help! For God's sake help! My wife….she's fallen ill…
please, someone, get help now!" he cried urgently to the faces
staring at the two of them. Soon people began appearing,
running towards them. One man pushed his way to the
front of the crowd. "I'm a doctor! Let me through please." He
immediately knelt down next to Emelia. She was breathing
with difficulty and making groaning sounds, but was unable
to talk. She was sweating profusely, even in the cool night
air. He listened to her chest, took her pulse, and looked
gravely at Bernardo.

"I think she has suffered a heart attack, señor. We must
get her to the hospital quickly!" He shouted to the crowd,
"Who will help me carry this woman to the car? She needs
to be taken to the hospital!" Several men stepped forward to
help Bernardo and the doctor lift her. One man supported
her arms, another her shoulders, another her legs and back.
Emelia weighed no more than 50 kilos, so she was virtually
weightless, but struggling for air and very pale. "Quickly!"
the doctor said, and pointed to the direction of the parking
lot down the boulevard. They were all in a careful run, like
a bizarre ballet of pallbearers, running in unison towards
the cars. The doctor raced ahead to a small blue Toyota in
the lot ahead. "Here. In here!" he said, as he fumbled with
his keys. "Put her in the back seat. Gently!" He opened
the rear doors of the car and the men gently eased Emelia's
limp body into the back of the car. "You, señor, please get

in the front with me. Hurry!" He jumped into the driver's side and started the car. Emelia's breathing was becoming erratic and infrequent. She was very pale. Bernardo felt as if he was floating, watching the scene as if it were happening to someone else. He was leaning sideways over the front seat, holding her limp hand and stroking it.

The men backed away as they slammed the rear doors shut and the doctor floored the car, driving violently towards the main road. "I know the way. We can be there in a matter of minutes!" Bernardo was not thinking or talking to this stranger, just watching his wife slipping away from life. He called her name softly, "Emelia, my darling. Stay with us. We're getting help. We'll be there soon." The car wove wildly through the hills up to the main road towards the Pan-American Highway. Soon lights, and a small hospital. The doctor sprang out of his car before it had even come to a full stop and ran for the emergency entrance. The car came to a rest with a slight thud against a small, sandy embankment. It seemed to be hours before anyone came out. Where were they?

Soon women in white, the doctor, and another man with a gurney were rushing towards the car. Emelia was hardly breathing at all. They gently pulled her from the back seat. One nurse began compressions on her chest as they raced back to the hospital entrance. Bernardo climbed out and began to run. He was floating; slowly his legs worked. He saw the people in white disappearing. He tried to run faster. Everything was in slow motion. He yelled, "Wait!" but it came out in a long deep "Wayyyyyyyyyyyyyyyyyyt!" He tried to run faster. His heart was beating faster and faster. He could hear it. He raised his arm to brush away the sweat. He was losing her! Where were they going??

Bernardo sat up in bed, startled, sweat covering his pajamas, the sheets, and the pillow. He was calling her name. It was dark. He was in his bedroom once again. He was exhausted, and full of sadness. The right side of the bed was empty. Her side. He held his head and wept. It was almost unbearable.

Once finished with the call with Victor, he had dug out his Beretta from the house safe and tucked it under his pillow. After the nightmare, Bernardo didn't sleep well at all. He tossed and turned the rest of the night, unable to get comfortable or find any peace. As the morning light began to appear, he decided that he might as well get out of bed and go downstairs for coffee. Part of him was still filled with overwhelming sadness from the dream of Emelia's death, and part was already waiting for Victor's call.

It was time to take action. He pulled his cell phone from his shirt pocket and dialed.

"Juan?" he said to a sleepy voice on the other end.

"Si, señor!" The voice suddenly became quite awake and at full attention.

"Please prepare my car, and call Geraldo and have him ready the jet. We will be going to Ancón. I'll be ready in an hour," he said, and hung up the cell.

Chapter Sixteen - Emelia

Emelia awoke with a pounding headache. She touched her temple with her right arm and felt a tug on the inside of her elbow. She opened her eyes and found herself staring at a blurry, bright-white ceiling. As her eyes became accustomed to the light, she noticed fluorescent lights and soundproofing panels where the bright white had been. The room spun lazily in circles. She felt sick, so she closed her eyes. Her breath seemed to be coming in gasps. There was a vague awareness of something that had happened to her, but her brain did not seem to be cooperating, except to let her know that she was in pain. She tried opening her eyes again. The brightness was almost overwhelming, but she forced her eyes around the room. Above her was an IV pole dripping some clear liquid into her right arm, which was taped to a board to keep it straight. Her left arm was restrained by something that held it firmly against whatever she was lying on. To her left was a door with a small window at the top. There were no windows to the outside. The room began to spin again. Her chest hurt when she took breaths. She shut her eyes and passed out.

She awoke with a start. She was cold and shivering. The IV was no longer in her right arm, and the headache was gone. There was an oxygen cannula in her nose, with a faint, cool breeze coming through it. The room had stopped spinning. A face with a funny white hat appeared over hers. She looked like a nurse.

"Ahh, señora, you're back with us, yes?" she asked in a quizzical, singsong way.

Emelia had no idea what she was talking about.

"Señora, you are in a hospital. My name is Maria, and I'm the nurse assigned to you for this shift. Are you aware of where you are?"

Emelia tried to talk, but nothing came out but a strange croaking sound. She hesitated, and then shook her head sideways.

"Señora, you are in a hospital in Santa Rosa. You came in last night after suffering heart failure due to curare poisoning. We have given you a drug called physostigmine and had to re-start your heart last night. It was very difficult to bring you back. When you arrived here you were clinically dead. Fortunately, the doctors revived you. You will have a difficult time talking for a while because your voice box is still a bit paralyzed, and you were on a respirator for quite a few hours. Let me get you some water." She reached over a poured a glass of water from a stainless steel pitcher, placed a straw in the glass, and raised Emelia up with one arm behind her back.

"Here. Drink. Just a sip. This will help."

Emelia accepted the water but felt exhausted. She could barely swallow the liquid and choked slightly, but it felt cool on her throat. She coughed again, losing some of the water.

"Slowly, slowly, señora, take your time," said the nurse in a reassuring manner. "We don't want you to drown after being poisoned!" She laughed at her own joke.

Emelia failed to see the humor in the comment. She was still trying to process the little information she had been given. Poisoned? She could not remember anything...no, she remembered having dinner with her husband, what was his name? She stared at the wedding ring on her left hand. She thought about kites. Were they flying kites when she was poisoned? She closed her eyes and saw girls running down a beach with a kite in their hands. It soared into the air. Emelia passed out again.

She was awakened by a man, gently shaking her shoulder.

"Emelia. Emelia. Can you wake up please?"

The voice seemed soft and warm.

"Emelia?"

She opened her eyes and saw a young man with a beard in a white coat leaning over her, staring into her eyes.

"Ahh, that's better!" he said with some animation. "Emelia, I'm Dr. Hong. I'm the doctor that has been assigned to your case. I would like to do a few tests to see how your reflexes are, OK?" Without waiting, he pulled a small flashlight out of his lab coat and flashed it in her eyes. It was bright and annoying.

"Good, good," he muttered, and grabbed her wrist, taking her pulse. After a few more minutes he put a stethoscope on and listened to her heart and lungs. "Breathe in please…and now breathe out…one more time, big breath…in….and out. Very good, señora. I'm almost finished."

He checked the blood pressure reading on the machine above her. He seemed satisfied based on the look on his face.

"Emelia, you have made an impressive recovery. Your vital signs all look good. Your lungs are clear, and your pulse and heart have returned to normal. For a woman of your age, you're in exceedingly good shape."

"Thank you," a voice that seemed to belong to Emelia said in return. She could talk! "How long have I been here?" she asked the doctor.

"Almost five days, señora, and lucky to be here at all, I might add." The doctor flipped through the chart at the end of Emelia's bed, made some notes, and was preparing to leave when Emelia stopped him. Five days?

"Wait!" she said. The doctor stopped and turned to her with a smile.

"Yes, Señora Villacorta? What can I do for you?"

Villacorta? That named suddenly jarred her brain back to the job of filling in the blanks. She was Emelia Podera Villacorta! She was married to Bernardo! She had been walking with him when suddenly she felt a slight prick on the back of her neck, and then terrible pain and pressure on her chest. She remembered being dragged and carried to a car and swerving off to somewhere...here? And then, nothing but darkness.

"Where is my husband?"

The doctor smiled at her and said, "Let me bring someone else in here to your room who can answer all your questions. I'm just the doctor." And with that, he opened the door and vanished.

Emelia fell asleep again. When she awoke, she felt very hungry. She looked over to the bedside table and saw a variety of foods; meats, cheese, vegetables, crackers, and bread. She propped herself up on her elbow and reached for the tray. She took some bread and stuffed it into her mouth. She drank some of the water to wash it down and then grabbed some fresh broccoli. She felt starved. The more she ate, the hungrier she got. Some salami, and more bread, a piece of tomato, and then lettuce. It all tasted so good! Her stomach began to roll. How long had it been since she had eaten? She paused to catch her breath, and sank back onto the bed.

She surveyed the room, really for the first time. It appeared to be a small hospital room with a closet and a door, probably leading to a bathroom, and her bed and bedside stand. The room was all white. There was no television and no phone. No windows and no clock in the room. Odd, she thought to herself. She had no idea what day it was, or whether it was day or night. All her jewelry, including her watch had been removed, all except her wedding band. She needed to get someone to come in to talk with her. She was feeling weak, but wanted to get up and use the bathroom. Railings were on both sides of her bed that did not allow her to swing her legs over the side. She saw a button hanging from the railing. She pushed it. Within a few seconds, a nurse appeared, dressed in white, with another one of those silly hats.

"Yes, señora. How can I help you?" she said with a smile.

"I would like to go to the bathroom please, but I think I'll need some help."

"Of course, señora. You may not remember, but we had a catheter in you while you were unconscious, however it has been removed." The nurse moved towards her bed, clicked something underneath, and the railing slid down.

"Here, let me help you sit up. I want you to just dangle your legs over the side of the bed until you feel as if you can walk," she said, as she slid an arm behind her and helped her sit up.

Emelia felt dizzy, but it passed.

"OK, let's go," she said, and the nurse grabbed underneath her right arm and supported her as her feet slid down to the floor.

"Good, señora!" the nurse encouraged.

Emelia shuffled her way towards the bathroom. It seemed to be miles away. She felt shaky and weak, but pushed forward, lifting one heavy foot after another. They reached the bathroom door and the nurse swung the door wide. Emelia suddenly noticed she was dressed in one of those gowns that left little to the imagination from behind.

"Let me back you in towards the toilet. You hold my hands and I'll help you sit down," the nurse said gently.

Emelia padded backwards a few steps and sat on the toilet. It was cold.

"All right, señora, I'll give you some privacy, but I'll be just outside this door. Let me know if you need help."

Emelia sat in the tiny fluorescent bathroom, shivering and trying to urinate. The whole experience was making her dizzy. She found her bladder finally working.

The nurse from outside the door said, "That is a great sign, señora! You're returning to life again! Are you finished? Do you need help?"

"No, no, I'm fine," and Emelia, wiping herself with awful institutional toilet paper, and reached to flush the toilet. She stood up and pivoted to the sink. Turning on the water, she began washing her hands, and suddenly was shocked by the vision she saw reflected back to her in the mirror above the sink. There was a woman who looked vaguely like her, disheveled hair, no makeup, and dark circles under her eyes. She looked drawn and pale.

"My God!" she said out loud. The nurse opened the door quickly to see what had happened.

"Oh, yes, I see you have not seen yourself for these past seven days. You have been through a lot, señora. Let's get your hands dried and get you back to bed."

The nurse took a clean towel and dried Emelia's hands, turned her towards the door, and pushed her gently in the direction of the bed.

After getting her comfortable, the nurse said she would send in someone to help her get cleaned up, and disappeared through the doorway out to the hall. Emelia briefly noticed that there did not seem to be anyone out in the hallway, but caught a glimpse of a drab green uniform of some kind, and an arm with a rifle sticking straight up in the air. The door clicked shut. She had the feeling she was locked in. She quickly fell asleep again.

CHAPTER SEVENTEEN

"Señora? Señora?"

Emelia felt herself being gently rocked from side to side. It was a female voice, one she did not recognize. For a moment she thought she was in her bed at home, but who would be disturbing her?

She opened her eyes to see a woman, young, perhaps in her twenties, staring back at her.

"Ahh, Señora Villacorta, you're finally awake!" said the smiling face. "I'm Sonia. I'm here to give you a little bath, and perhaps we can put on a little makeup, brush your hair and your teeth…." She did not wait for an answer, but moved a table towards the bed. It had a large stainless steel bowl, and a few washcloths and towels. Before Emelia could respond, Sonia began helping her remove her hospital gown, and began placing the washcloths in the bowl.

"This will make you feel a lot better, señora," Sonia said, as she slowly cleansed Emelia's entire body with a warm, soapy solution. It felt great and smelled pleasant. Emelia just complied and said nothing, but began to collect her thoughts. As the female voice droned on about the weather and how nice it was this time of year, Emelia began to mentally take stock of what her situation was. She felt stronger, and clear for the first time that she could remember since awakening here. Questions began to fall into a list in her head. Where was she? Why hadn't Bernardo come to see her? Were these people really who they said they were? Why had she been poisoned? What was the end game here? Where were her clothes and belongings? When could she leave? Could she use her phone? Why were there apparently guards outside her door?

"So, you're all cleaned up now, señora," the voice said. "Let me brush out your hair. Here is a toothbrush and some toothpaste for you." She slid them over with a small bowl and a glass of water.

Emelia brushed her teeth and spit the water into the bowl. She rinsed her mouth with the cool water and spit into the bowl again. Sonia was right, she did feel better.

Sonia gathered up the items she had brought with her and headed for the door. She rapped on the small slit of a window three times. A lock was turned from the outside, and the door swung open. A guard was clearly allowing only Sonia to pass. Sonia said over her shoulder as she left, "There are some things on the chair beside your bed for you to wear. Please put them on. I'll return with the doctor in a little while."

The door slammed shut, and Emelia was alone in the sterile, cold room. Shivering slightly, she swung her legs to the side of the bed and reached for the pile of clothing on the chair. There was underwear, *cheap cotton*, she noted to herself, and a dress that looked too large and fairly old. No matter, it was clothing. Emelia got dressed.

Within fifteen minutes there was a knock at the door, a courtesy she thought absurd considering she was in a locked room with a guard outside.

"Señora?

"Yes," Emelia replied in a soft voice.

"Señora, this is Dr. Hong. May I come in?"

"Of course," said Emelia. The formality was a bit comical, in view of her circumstances.

The door lock clacked and opened, revealing a smiling Dr. Hong in a white lab coat. Sonia, the nurse who had bathed her earlier was with him, as well as another man in a dark blue suit. They came into the room muttering quietly to each other; she could only pick up parts of sentences. The words "better" and "improved," "color" and "ready for"… something, she couldn't quite make it out. They gathered around her bed, studying her. Dr. Hong pulled a stethoscope from around his neck and inserted the two ends into his ears, leaning towards her.

"If I could just listen to your heart and lungs, please. This will only take a moment." He placed his stethoscope on her chest, just over her heart, and listened. He smiled and asked her to take a few deep breaths, and then smiled again.

"Your heart and lungs sound fine; strong, and no congestion in the lungs." He reached for her inside wrist.

"Just a quick check of the pulse…."

After about thirty seconds of staring at his watch, he proclaimed her well. He stepped back from the bed and the man in the suit came forward, extending his right hand.

"Señora Villacorta. Allow me to introduce myself. You may remember me, my name is Sr. Luis Castellano. I'm the head of Research and Development for GMBI. Perhaps you remember us? It's an honor to meet you. I'm familiar with your work. Very impressive."

Emelia recoiled slightly, and did not accept the handshake. Luis looked a bit put off, but only for a moment, and then regained his composure.

"No? Well, that's understandable. You've been through a lot. I'm sure you have many questions. We'll meet later today and discuss all these things and more." He backed away, muttered something out of the corner of his mouth to the doctor, and started for the door.

"Wait!" Emelia's voice was more urgent than she had wanted it to sound. "Am I being kept here against my will? Just what exactly is going on?" She could feel her cheeks flushing with anger. She was no longer a victim. She wanted answers— now. She stood up and moved towards the group. They in turn knocked on the door three times, and as it swung open, they scurried through the open doorway.

"Don't let her out!" the doctor shouted to the guard, and slammed the door shut. Emelia heard the bolt swing through the frame, locking the door. She felt dizzy, and sat down on the bed again. GMBI? R&D? What were these people up to? How did this Castellano man know about her work? She felt fear starting to creep into her mind. She shook it off. *I need to focus. I need to find a way out, to get ahold of Bernardo, but how?* She studied the room and walked into the bathroom. Solid walls, thick bolted doors, very small air vents. There was not any easy way to escape from this room. Even the electrical outlets had been covered and were locked. Emelia sat back on her bed, sighed, and waited to see what came next.

A fairly well-built, older man entered the room with the ease and warm smile acquired from years of glad handing. He reached out to take her small hands in his. His light brown hair flecked with gray, blue eyes, and six-foot stature advertised *American* all over, which was confirmed when he spoke to her.

"Emeelyah, I am so glad to finally meet ya after all these years. I'm Bob Parks."

Emelia was stunned. The voice, of course, sounded familiar from many conversations over the phone, but she had never really seen him before. He was, in his own way, an attractive man. Emelia managed to blurt out an awkward response.

"Mr. Parks! What...ah...I...what are you doing here? What is this place? Why are you here? I don't understand what's going on...what..." She felt faint again and sat back down on the bed, bracing herself against the mattress.

"Oh, I'm sure it is confusing," Parks said empathically. "I had heard through our channels that you were severely ill, and felt it imperative that I come down here on the first plane from St. Louis when I got the news. We have shared so much over the years, Emeelyah (he said in a transparent phoniness), I feel as if I'm a member of the family. And when family's having trouble, well, we come a-runnin'." He smiled a perfectly white-toothed smile that, for some reason, reminded her of the Cheshire Cat in "Alice in Wonderland." Americans. They really had an obsession with "Movie Star Teeth."

"How's Bernardo?" *Asked and answered*, she thought to herself.

Emelia was understandably confused. Did Bob not know what was going on here? He had to. So what was he up to? She decided to play along. Her mind began to return to its usual sharpness. Smile, observe, say as little as possible, and play the distraught female role. She ignored his question about her husband and went straight to the point.

"Bob, I have no idea what's going on here. I feel as if I'm being held captive in this place, but I don't understand…" (Voice trailing off). *Look confused and distraught,* she thought to herself. *Get straight to the point,* she thought. She burned with the flush of betrayal…

"Bob, Mr. Parks, can you get me out of here?" Why not go for the "brass ring."

"Well, ya know, Emelia, that's why I'm here. And right now that's a bit of a problem. Ya see, these guys in the company have this idea that you may know more than you're sayin', and I gotta be honest, I think you do too, followin' your research an' all. So, the best thing you can do, to help yourself out in this situation, you know what I mean, is to ah…cooperate. I can guarantee your safety, and a quick release from this place if you just "play ball" with the guys that are gonna be talkin' to ya, you know what I mean?"

Emelia nodded her head. It seemed as if words were pointless at this juncture.

"Well, all right then." Bob smiled a bright, toothy smile. "I guess we have a deal then." He extended his hand out to Emelia's as if they had just consummated a large business deal. She took his hand and shook it. He squeezed a little too hard, making her wince.

"So, it's been great to see ya, Emelia. I'll let these other guys talk with ya now, and we'll hook up for breakfast or something real soon, OK? Say hi to Bernardo." It seemed as if he couldn't get out of the room fast enough. And with that, he turned to the door, rapped three times, the guard opened the door, and he was gone.

After what she imagined were several hours passing, the door to her room abruptly swung open and a guard motioned to her.

"Come with me, please," he said, his right hand resting slightly on the holstered pistol on his hip.

"Where are we going?" Emelia asked.

"Just come with me, señora, please." The tone was quite final.

Emelia went to the soldier, and he escorted her down a hallway. There were no other people anywhere that she could see. It looked as if it was an abandoned corridor in a hospital. They moved to an elevator, the door shut, the guard pressed "1," and they descended to the first floor. The door opened again, and the guard gently grabbed her elbow and moved her out of the elevator and down another hallway, also empty. Emelia decided there was no point in asking any more questions, since her escort clearly was not in a talking mood.

They arrived at an office door with frosted glass concealing what was inside. The guard knocked three times (apparently a universal code), and a voice from inside said, "Come in."

Inside there was a desk, papers neatly organized on top, several comfortable chairs, volumes of books on the wall from floor to ceiling, and Luis Castellano seated behind the desk.

"Please, señora, sit down." He motioned to a chair in front of the desk. He looked at the guard.

"You may wait outside. Thank you."

The guard did a crisp about-face, and without a word, let himself out and closed the door behind him. Emelia could see his large shadow, standing at attention, through the frosted glass.

"So," Luis began, "You must have many questions, which I'll be happy to answer, Señora Villacorta. However, I probably should tell you a few important things before we proceed."

Emelia simply stared at him.

"Most importantly, you're dead, at least as far as the rest of the world, including your husband, are concerned." His words hit her like a punch to the chest, knocking some of the air out of her.

"In fact, Bernardo was just here yesterday retrieving your ashes from your cremation. Such a tragedy. We did our best to comfort him. Well, not me exactly, but the staff, many of whom you have already met."

Emelia felt a flush rising in her face. Her husband had been here? She forced herself to remain silent.

"So that is point number one. As a dead person, the world, as far as you're concerned, has moved on. You don't exist. Which brings me to point number two. We, I should say my company, are aware of the work you have been doing to try to develop a hybrid code to neutralize the patented process we're using in all of our hybrid GMO products. To be perfectly blunt about it, señora, we cannot allow that to happen. There is just too much money at stake.

"Finally, and this is probably the most important piece of information for you, personally, is your future—or lack of it. We're prepared to relocate you to another country where you can start a new life. You will be well provided for, and can live out your remaining days in comfort...in exchange for your research notes and any product you may have already developed. So, any questions for me?" Luis said, smiling.

Emelia already knew what lay ahead. The only reason she was actually still alive was that they hadn't found her research, nor would they. Her laboratory, years of work, and seeds were buried in the bowels of the earth, underneath an intricately protected and disguised location in their hacienda in Ancón. She also knew it was just a matter of time before they ran out of patience. She needed to get out of this place, wherever it was, get back to her laboratory, and warn Bernardo; but how? She stared back at Luis defiantly.

"I have a friend, a very powerful friend, who will show no mercy to any of you once he finds out about this, this... ridiculous sham you're putting on here. Do you think I'm at your mercy? You're insane!" she shouted back at him.

"Oh," Luis smiled back at her again, feigning concern. "You must be talking about General de la Hoya." Emelia was astonished that he knew who she was talking about.

"Yes. The general brought your husband the news of your... demise. We will be meeting in Ica in the next week to finalize our discussions with the Minister of Agriculture. Yes, indeed, he's a very powerful man, and a good friend to

your husband and family, and…one of the best liars I have
ever met!"

Emelia was stunned. *Victor?* Her paranoia began to increase
by the moment. Who else was involved in this? Bernardo
must be warned. Ica? Why Ica? What meeting?

"I can see you have many thoughts on your mind now. I
trust I haven't upset you too much, señora. This is a lot to
take in. Now, you have many questions for me, yes?"

Emelia's fiery brown eyes stared back at him, her lips pressed
thin with contempt. She had to buy time, to make a plan.
First she had to relax. She envisioned the hacienda in Cuzco,
surrounded by the snow-capped Andes Mountains in the
Valle Sagrado. It was a meditation exercise she had learned
long ago. It gave her peace. She let out her breath slowly.

"I'll need some time to consider your offer," Emelia said,
calming herself. "I have no questions at the moment."

"I'll give you twenty-four hours, señora. After that, the offer
will be withdrawn, and you really will die, but not before
some very painful procedures are performed on you that
are guaranteed to extract the information we need. I would
like to avoid this unpleasantness, as I'm sure, would you. I'm
impressed that you have taken this new information so well.

So, fine, take some time to consider the offer. We will meet again tomorrow. Now, if there is nothing more to discuss, I'll have you escorted back to your room." Luis rose from his seat and called to the guard outside the door.

The guard took her elbow again and gently ushered her out the door and down the corridor. She saw a stainless steel cart in the hallway, just before they got to the elevator. As they neared it, she noticed a few surgical instruments on top. She suddenly fell to her knees, gripping her stomach with one hand, and reached onto the cart with the other, as if to brace herself. She collapsed, groaning, and spilled the contents of the cart onto the floor as the guard struggled to help her.

"Oh!" she exclaimed. "Please, just a moment." The guard was following her down to the floor, forgetting his hold on his pistol in an attempt to help the woman from hitting her head on the hard floor.

Emelia spotted just what she was looking for and grabbed it in one swift move. It was a large surgical clamp, which she grabbed around the base where the fingers were usually inserted, and in a single violent thrust, plunged the end into the jugular vein of the soldier's neck, causing massive amounts of blood to squirt out of his throat. He cried out in pain, released his hold on Emelia, and instinctively grabbed for his throat. Emelia then thrust the instrument through the inside of his pants leg, near his groin, severing the femoral artery and causing another massive hemorrhage. Blood was everywhere. The soldier took only 30 seconds to lose consciousness, and bled out completely in less than a minute.

Emelia looked up to see if anyone had noticed the commotion. She was covered in blood spatter, and surrounded by a huge pool of red on the terrazzo floor. Silence. She scrambled to her feet. There was no time to clean up the mess, she was sure of that. She grabbed the soldier's pistol, a Glock 19, cocked it back into the ready position, and ran down the hallway in search of an exit. As she ran, she noticed a white jacket and a surgical cap on a hook near one of the doors. She grabbed both and put them on over her bloody clothing and hair. Behind her, there were bloody footsteps on the hall floor. She kicked off her shoes and ran down the hall. There had to be a way out of there. She knew she was on the first floor because the guard had pressed "1" in the elevator. She ran to the right, and saw daylight streaming out behind a set of double doors.

She heard muffled voices in the distance beyond the double doors. To her left was a bathroom. She ducked inside to look at the disguise she had created. Staring back at her from the mirror was a disheveled looking woman, dressed in a lab coat, with a cap shoved down over her hair. She straightened the cap, buttoned up the lab coat, and quickly washed her bloody hands and took a towel to wipe off the blood spatter on her face. She pinched her cheeks, combed her hair with her fingers, wondered about being barefoot, and rushed back into the hallway. It would have to do. The Glock in her lab coat pocket banged intrusively into her hip as she pushed through the double doors. She scanned the hallway in front of her. A few nurses behind a desk, what appeared to be other hospital staff in white were walking, and ahead, two doors to the outside! She could see brown mountains, and a parking lot in the distance.

Emelia took a deep breath and walked purposefully towards the outside doors. Nobody even looked up. An ambulance had just arrived. People were brushing by her to get to the waiting techs. She exited the building as the nurse and ambulance techs were lifting some poor woman onto a gurney and heading back inside. She walked by, closed the back doors of the empty ambulance, and slid into the driver's seat. The motor was still running. She put the vehicle in drive, and slowly slid out the circular road to the main street ahead. *Don't be in a hurry,* she said to herself, marveling at what had just happened in the last two or three minutes. Her heart was pumping so hard she thought it was going to break out of her chest. She slowed her breathing, turned on the signal indicator, and drove off down the street.

To her amazement, she was in Santa Rosa. She knew the small town well, and even better, her own hacienda in Ancón was only a few minutes away. She sped up and headed for the brown hills of Ancón.

Chapter Eighteen - Ancón

The flight from Cuzco to Ancón was about an hour and three quarters. Towards the end of the flight, the jet began to bank left and descend, and Bernardo realized they were approaching a very remote and discreet landing strip. As they banked past the familiar landmark of Las Olas Golpeando (literally "pounding waves"), he saw familiar rock cliffs lining the Pacific Ocean, and then the aircraft turned inland towards Santa Rosa. There was an abandoned racetrack there with just enough straightaway to land a Gulfstream G150, about 1,524 meters. The tricky part was not getting to the end before the sharp bank of the racetrack to the left. As usual, they landed with room to spare, and the pilot quickly turned the jet around and taxied to a small hangar.

A car was waiting for Bernardo as he stepped out into the cool weather. He got in and told the driver, "To my hacienda in Ancón."

The car sped off to the north. All around this seaside area was the contradiction of an empty range of brown mountains and drifts of sand, with not a speck of life to the horizon out of his right window, and to the left, the vast reaches of the Pacific. The car left the main road within a few miles and headed up into the brown, dusty hills of Ancón. Then, after a few more miles of brown desolation, a mirage appeared. A large white house, surrounded by trees, grass, colorful flowers, and shrubs, with an equally impressive high steel fence with ribbon and electrical wire around the top and bottom of the fence, with the familiar yellow sign with black skull and crossbones, "Peligro!" Certain death would occur from the electricity, the ribbon wire, and the sharpshooters. This hacienda was unlike the one in Cuzco. This area, while safe many years ago, had now been overrun with squatters from the cities, who simply took what they wanted. Peruvian law was still in effect; if a person could sustain himself for five years on a piece of property in this "wilderness" of brown sand where nothing grew, then it was his property. Bernardo would have none of that. Anyone who was unfortunate enough to try was asked once, and once only, to not return. It was made very clear that this was a big desert; big enough to find some land somewhere else, or big enough to never be found again. Very few people ever ventured this far into the desert anymore.

As Bernardo's car approached the gates swung open, and the car drove up a steep driveway to the hacienda. It was as if they had been transported to another planet. Life was everywhere. Birds, lizards, flowers, fruit trees, fountains, and the beautiful home that he and Emelia designed and had constructed. The landscaping was all Emelia, and it was breathtaking. Small gardens and carefully tended bougainvillea of all colors were scattered around the property. It was a paradise that should not have existed. Bernardo's geology background and research had discovered that underneath all this brown, ugly sand, and about another mile of the same rock they had just flown over coming into Santa Rosa, was a vast underground aquifer of the purest water he had ever seen or tasted. So, in a land of desolation, there lay this tiny island of utopia.

He got out of the car, grabbing his few belongings. As he entered the house, he was greeted by the housekeeper, Mariana, and a small staff of women.

"We missed you when you were here last week, señor." And then realizing that he had been here burying his wife, she blushed, and cast her eyes to the floor. "I'm so sorry, señor.

That was so thoughtless of me. Please forgive my stupidity. We're all so saddened by the loss of the señora."

"It's all right, Mariana," said Bernardo with a sigh. "I, too, would like not to think of it anymore." He briskly walked up the stairs to his bedroom, saying over his shoulder, "Please wake me for dinner. Something light, and some red wine, please."

Bernardo had no intention of sleeping. He would change into lighter clothing and use the closet to go down the very private stairway to an equally private passage underground to another place of even more astounding offerings. It was not an accident that this hacienda was located where it was in the seeming desolation of brown. Long ago, Bernardo had discovered this storehouse from yet another quipu that he had deciphered.

He opened the door in his bedroom to a spacious closet filled with clothes, both his and Emelia's. Hats, and coats, shirts and slacks, dresses, and every imaginable type of shoe, all neatly ordered and carefully placed in the expansive closet. In the center of the closet was a jewelry case, much the same as one might see in a jewelry store. In fact, that was where it had come from; a Lima jewelry store—with a few modifications. The upper pane of glass was bulletproof and three inches thick, as were the glass walls surrounding the case. Inside was a collection of gold and jewels that rivaled those of any king or queen; gifts to Emelia over the years. Ironically, the whole case was valueless to both of them, since they knew that thousands of times this much jewelry could be replaced in a few days. There was a sophisticated alarm system attached, and one simple key that turned the entire system on and off. Left to lock and arm, right to unlock and disarm, and right again to get to the real valuables. This would release the door in the rear of the closet that led to the stairway. The jewelry case was really a ruse. If someone *was* somehow lucky enough to get into the case, the contents would be the focus, not anything more. Bernardo had learned this lesson a long time ago; leave what is hidden in full view, and it will never be found.

He went to his selection of ties and found the one he was looking for, a nondescript navy blue tie with red spots. He removed it from the rack. Attached to it was a tie clip in the shape of a Nazca spider in plain silver, with no other decoration. It actually looked like something that would be sold in the local tourist market. He unclipped the clasp, turned it over, and revealed a complex toothed key that could easily be mistaken for the clasp side of the tie clip. Overlook the obvious...Bernardo put the key into the jewelry case and turned right once; he heard the click of the alarm shutting off. Then right once again to hear a release in the rear of the closet. He removed the "key" and put the clip back on the tie, returned it to the rack, and walked to the rear of the closet. As he pushed through the opening, cool air flowed out of the entrance. He hit a light switch on the right side of the entrance, and a long line of lights descended down the stairs and into the darkness. He pulled the door shut behind him and began to go down the stone stairs.

Bernardo was a great believer in redundancy. On the outside chance that someone got this far, they would find at the end of this long, damp, and extremely cool stone tunnel, an elaborate wine cellar. The cellar itself was magnificent, containing rows and rows of very old wines from all over the world, quite dusty, and an occasional bottle missing for authenticity. There were wine glasses neatly stored in a beautiful mahogany cabinet, and a marble-topped tasting table in the center of the small room. Surrounding the room were racks from knee height to the ceiling, filled with wines of all colors and bottle sizes.

On the third row facing the entrance, at the top of the left side rack, was a Château Latour 1964 Bordeaux, probably worth $700 a bottle. On the right was an oddity, a Tacama Malbec; not that old, but still dusty. He reached up and pulled the Malbec out of its rack. It was a heavy bottle, filled with sand, and released the entire rack with a slight click. The rack was balanced perfectly, and swung open to reveal yet another set of stairs descending into the cool darkness. He groped for the light switch on the wall and, turning it on, revealed another line of lights that led down the stairway. Bernardo closed the rack gently behind him and continued his descent.

At the bottom of the stairway, the tunnel widened and sparkled with typical Inca gold foil covering the walls and ceiling. Its beauty never failed to thrill him. All round him were elaborate carvings telling stories in pictures, of the people that had once proudly been the owners of this land. Room upon room were filled with artifacts, from simple plates, cups and pitchers, to more elaborate statues and weavings, and of course, gold, silver, and jewels, fashioned into exquisite decorative trees, birds, and animals. Bernardo had long ago lost interest in the actual value of these things, but had grown to appreciate and love the intricate design and craftsmanship in each and every thing he had discovered. Examples of that craftsmanship could still be seen in many of the old Catholic churches built on the backs of the Inca people before the Spanish conquistadores had slaughtered them.

Bernardo walked down the hallway until he got to a room on the right with a large golden condor perched on a golden log over the threshold. Its large wings spanned the entire width of the entrance. This room had been turned into Emelia's private study and storage area. All along the well-lit walls were glass vials of various seeds, with labels and numbers on them. On top of the old ironwood desk in the center of the room were notebooks and papers, and of course, her old Royal typewriter and favorite fountain pen. Typewriter! He sat at the desk and scrolled a piece of paper into the roller and typed. Some of the letters were partially filled in with ink, especially the *o*'s. He noticed the same with the *e* and the *a*. There was suddenly no doubt in his mind that this was the very same typewriter that had been used to make the list. Emelia? She typed this?

Lying to the side of the typewriter was an article, more like an official memorandum, with the GMBI logo at the top and the word *Classified* watermarked diagonally across it. He picked up the document and scanned it rapidly. It appeared to be, in part, pieces of an article that had been published online several years ago. In the margins, Emelia's familiar handwriting had made notes, the first of which was in bright red: "Kiwicha!!!" and another word: "Amaranth." He scanned the memo.

What Emelia had apparently discovered in her research was that Amaranth had cross bred with other crops, resulting in a new seed crop no longer a GMO, but resistant to GMBI's powerful herbicides without the threat of lawsuit or copyright infringement due to its altered DNA. Pachamama, in her wisdom has supplied a way out, not to mention Kiwicha itself, which was a grain, potent in protein and antioxidants. He was stunned to see that GMBI had know this since 2005 and had encouraged their farmers to pull up the Amaranth plants as best they could, since they had extremely deep root systems. GMBI advised the increase of heavier dosages of glyphosate, and another shocker, enhance it with the use of "Agent Orange", used as a defoliant during the Vietnam War. That must be good for you, Bernardo thought, shaking his head from side to side.

Stunned, he lay the memo down and began to realize what pages had been removed from her notebooks, and why. This information alone was proof positive that GMBI's failures in the United States were spreading around the world, threatening the entire GMO industry. No wonder they were so rabid about getting a deal signed in Peru! And they were apparently willing to stop at nothing short of murder to make the deal happen.

Was Emelia taking this substance from Kiwicha, and cloning it into other seeds?

Bernardo took the list that he'd gotten from Victor out of his shirt pocket and studied the numbers and letters. He had a strong hunch that there was a connection here. He listened once again to that "little "...voice" in his head that directed him to make decisions, which at times seemed crazy. Rarely was he wrong. Call it instinct, or intuition, or something more spiritual, Bernardo listened and acted. He looked at the first two numbers; 34H31 and 33P67. Knowing Emelia, if these numbers had anything to do with what he was thinking, the vials would be in numerical order. He started at his far left and shined a small flashlight on the vials: 21A03, 21A04, 21B16, 22C38, and so on. He saw the numbers rise as he moved around the room. Scanning... scanning...33W16, 33C76, 33P67! There was the first one. He gently lifted it off the shelf and placed it on the desk. As he moved further around the room, he found another, 34H31. He removed that one as well, and set it on the desk. Tucking the piece of paper back in his shirt pocket, he knew he had found what he was looking for. He sat down in the upholstered chair at the desk and opened the vial marked 33P67. Inside there were seeds, but there was also a tightly rolled paper scroll. He gently extracted the scroll. The paper was fairly new, still white. He unrolled the tiny scroll and began to read.

My darling Bernardo, if you have found this message then you have followed the breadcrumbs well! You are in grave danger, my love. These seeds and others you will discover, as well as other messages, are very valuable, and worth killing for. Some may have died already. Please be careful and trust no one, especially Victor. I love you, my darling. Emelia

Bernardo fell back against the chair and found it hard to breathe. His mind was spinning. Seeds? Victor? Was Emelia talking to him from the grave? His heart was pounding in his chest, and it suddenly felt warm in the room. He took a deep breath, and reached for the second vial. In it, too, were another type of seed; these looked like corn of some sort, and another tiny scroll. He unrolled it and read:

> *My darling Bernardo, I must warn you of Miguel Montoya. If he is still alive, I may not have been successful. He's working with GMBI on a deal to plant corn crops that are GMOs all over Peru. I was involved in these discussions and objected to the idea. Once I explained privately to Miguel what would happen, that GMBI would eventually control our food source, he went against me immediately. Some of these seeds are proof of what they intend to do. They are modified to resist herbicides, and will produce tenfold what normal corn would. The have also been patented and protected and made infertile. This is not known by anyone except GMBI. My research has been devoted to countering this with a secret weapon of sorts…too complicated to explain. More to come, your adoring wife, Emelia*

He took another deep breath and pulled the list from his shirt pocket. Bernardo got up from his chair, and one by one, retrieved the remaining vials on the list. In the back of his mind, he thought the disguise was brilliant. There had to be literally hundreds and hundreds of vials in this room. Without the code, no information. And so, one by one he read the contents of Emelia's secrets. The scrolls named names, locations, dates, and meeting times of many secret meetings with GMBI. There were a lot of crops involved: Maize, quinoa, kiwicha, wheat, barley, soy beans; even coffee and cacao beans. Of all the entries he read, the most chilling was in 42P56:

> *….my life is also in jeopardy, my darling. They know I hold the key to all this information and will stop at nothing to get it suppressed. I may be dead by the time you read this. You must get this information out to the people. Los Cóndores de Oro is in the middle of this whole thing. They will be approaching you at some time. Trust no one…I love you, Emelia*

CHAPTER NINETEEN - VICTOR

General Victor de La Hoya stared intently at a color map of his country, with a small blue dot pulsating on his 19" flat computer screen. He always prided himself on having the very best in technology. This was a Dell, made in the United States, and very expensive. Occasionally one or two would "disappear" in a shipment to some corporation in Lima and, as if by some strange stroke of luck, appear in his office, still in their original packaging. He used his mouse to zoom in on the map. *What the hell?* he thought to himself. As he zoomed in closer to the pulsing blue dot, the topography became more complex. Roads appeared, buildings sprang up, and then the names of the roads and the towns. Ancón?

He zoomed in further. The blue dot was pulsing in the hills of Ancón, but there were no discernable buildings, just landscape and hills and rocks. *What the hell is Bernardo doing up there?* he thought to himself. That lying bastard!

We just dragged his ass out of that town not more than two weeks ago, and now he's back there again.... He grabbed for his cell and called Bernardo. After five rings, there was an answer.

"Hello? Victor? What's going on? I was busy, sorry I didn't get to the phone more quickly." Bernardo had re-emerged from the tunnel to the rooms below the hacienda just in time, it would seem.

Victor steadied his voice. "Bernardo. Just called to see how you're doing. How are things in Cuzco?"

"Oh fine, fine," he lied. "I've just been thinking; I should really go to that meeting in Ica next Monday."

The general's blood began to boil. So, we're playing cat and mouse now, are we? He measured his words carefully. "Yes, I'll be there of course, my friend, wouldn't miss it; but I thought I told you not to go? This could be a very dangerous meeting. I haven't seen the agenda yet, but I heard from some of our friends there would be important things to discuss, things that do not concern you, my friend. I thought I made that clear. Have you heard anything different?"

"No, nothing. But I really must disagree with you, and I insist that I come. I think I have some important information to share with the others," he lied again. What was Victor up to? He wondered what the real purpose of the call was.

"We will discuss Ica later. I'm very busy right now. By the way, the real reason for my call was to check to see if my men made it to your house OK. We should keep them there until the trip next week, if you insist on coming; just for your safety, of course." A silence. "Bernardo? Are you there?"

Damn! Bernardo had completely forgotten about the soldiers Victor had said he would send to "guard" the house. "Uh, no, you know, Victor, they haven't arrived yet. Perhaps they got delayed…the weather has been bad here. Very windy and overcast." He was stalling; it even sounded like he was stalling.

"What?" said Victor, with immodest shock in his voice. He clenched the mouse in his hand so hard it started to crack. "I gave very clear instructions for them to be there by now. This is bullshit! I'll make some inquiries now. Leave it to me, my friend; heads are going to roll!" *He's lying to me? Me?*

"Victor, this really isn't necessary. Besides, I'm thinking of going back to Lima, maybe as early as this afternoon. Please, just call it off. I hope it doesn't inconvenience them too much." Was this going to fly? *Probably not,* he thought to himself. Victor was anything but stupid.

Suddenly there was a low rumbling on the earpiece of Bernardo's phone.

"What the hell?" Victor said, a little unnerved. Bernardo heard things breaking, and more roaring in the earpiece, and then sirens.

"Bernardo, I'll have to call you back. *Terremoto* (earthquake)." He abruptly hung up the phone. Earthquakes were relatively common in Peru, and could vary in intensity. This one was big. Everything was vibrating and shaking. The palace was being shuddered to its very foundations. Little waterfalls of dust were falling onto his beloved computer, his desk, and his head. The stone floor seemed to literally be rolling, which seemed at face value, impossible.

He got up from his chair and waddled to the door, staggering from the floor movement, which made him look drunk, not that anyone was looking. Sirens were going off all over the building. He heard people yelling; "Terremoto! Terremoto!" Where the hell was his staff? *Bastards*, he thought to himself, as he struggled to open the door. He had learned a long time ago that in situations like this, panic overtook nearly everyone. Heroics were for the newscasts. Everyone headed for the streets and away from buildings, even though nearly every building in Lima was made to withstand earthquakes of magnitude 7.5; that is, the modern ones were. The palace was not a modern building, but still, they knew a thing or two about earthquakes even when this was built. He knew he'd get out, and then take care of this Bernardo thing once and for all.

Victor pulled at the old solid cedar door. It would not budge. He yanked on the old brass doorknob harder, dust settling all around him in small clouds. His heart was beginning to beat faster. The thick door did not budge. Nothing. Breathing in the cloudy air made the work more difficult. He pulled again, this time with all his weight leaning backwards, right foot braced against the doorframe. Dust spilled onto his shiny black boots and down to the stone floor. "Mierda!" he puffed, coughing. Then, as if the door responded to the curse, the knob came loose in his hand and he sprang backwards, arms flailing, trying desperately to catch his balance.

General Victor de la Hoya struck the back of his head on the edge of his thick oak desk, perfectly transecting the spinal cord and rendering him immediately a quadriplegic, cutting off nerve supply to the heart and lungs. His last thought? *Fuck me!* He collapsed onto the floor like a cow hit by a stunner, instantly brain dead. His blank eyes stared unblinking up into the dust settling on them. Within two minutes, the general stopped breathing, and his lifeless, grotesquely large corpse lay in the dust.

CHAPTER TWENTY

Bernardo felt the tremors from the earthquake almost immediately as the phone went dead. The house shook and the ground seemed to vibrate with an intensity that made him worried. He raced down the stairs of the hacienda only to find his small staff already huddled outside the house in the driveway, holding each other and studying the house to see what would happen. Some of the women were crying. More important in Bernardo's mind, looking to the east, was the chance of a tsunami. It really depended on the location of the quake. If it was offshore, the chances were greater. A tsunami would be of no consequence in their location high in the hills, but all along the beaches and coastline there were signs posted of tsunami hazard zones. While there had not been much significant activity in central Peru since 1996, Bernardo knew his history as a geologist. On October 28, 1746, an earthquake hit and was reportedly the largest to strike central Peru in recorded history. This magnitude 8.0

to 8.6 quake completely destroyed the cities of Lima, Callao, Chancay, and everything else along the central Peruvian coast. Reportedly half an hour following the shock, a large tsunami struck the shore with 80-meter tidal waves, causing great damage at all Peruvian ports, and killing thousands.

He grabbed his field glasses from a small desk at the entrance to the house and walked calmly to the edge of the driveway, scanning the coastline below. The waters seemed relatively calm. The usual telltale sign was a rapid contraction of the sea, usually exposing large areas of land that would normally be completely covered by water, even at low tide. And then moments later, a wall of water would rush back towards the shore. The trembling was continuing to subside. He had not heard the tsunami warning sirens, but through his glasses, he could see large crowds of men, women, and children running towards high ground. They knew better, and did not need sirens to warn them of impending disaster.

He walked calmly over to his staff huddled in the front of the house, fear in their eyes. Someone had switched on a small radio, and the announcer was speaking rapidly. Apparently the quake was registered as a 5.8, 41 kilometers from Lima, near the coast. While that was bad in terms of potential damage, it was good in terms of no tsunami. He spoke to his staff in a calm, gentle manner.

"Apparently this earthquake was not that serious. We will be all right. If you need to go and tend to your families to make sure they are safe, please do so. I'll be fine here by myself. Please be careful, and remember that there are almost always aftershocks. There is plenty of room here on the grounds for you and your families to stay until you feel secure. Now, please go, if you feel the need."

Seven of the nine staff grabbed a few meager belongings and headed down the driveway towards town. Only Bernardo's driver and a housekeeper remained.

"Will you be needing a ride anywhere soon, señor?"

"No, not right now, but thank you. Please feel free to go back into the house and get something to eat or drink. It's perfectly safe, I assure you."

"Gracias, señor," he said, and he and the housekeeper walked towards the hacienda. The trembling had stopped, at least for now.

Bernardo's mind turned again to the conversation with Victor. He must have known he was lying to him about where he was, and it was only a matter of time before he called back and continued his obtuse line of questioning. He smiled to himself and thought, *Never thought I'd be happy about an earthquake...* A sudden thought occurred to him. When they had arrived at the landing strip, he had been rushed into his car. He was in such a hurry, he never performed his usual sweep of any vehicle he got into. He fumbled in the pocket of his jacket and found the GPS tracker device indicator he always carried with him. It was small, only about the size of half a pack of cigarettes, and of course, turned off! He walked towards the Mercedes and pushed the "On" button to the device. Immediately it indicated that his car was being tracked. Bernardo got down on his knees and ran his hand along the inside of the rear bumper. Nothing. He went to the front of the car and performed the same task. Nothing. He leaned over the passenger side wheel well and ran his hand inside the curve of the metal. Bingo! He pulled on the small metal box and it released its magnetic hold on the vehicle. Green light. It was active. *Mierda!* Bernardo thought to himself.

So, Victor had known exactly where he was when they were talking just a few minutes ago! He reached into his other pocket and pulled out his cell phone and turned it off. He dropped the tracking device on the drive and stomped hard on the box with his heel. The light went off. Just to be sure, he took the carcass of the GPS tracker and dumped it unceremoniously into the fountain. How much time did he have? Bernardo settled his mind, and thought methodically. Lima...earthquake...some degree of chaos there. Military would be involved in rescue and cleanup operations. Traffic will be even more than the usual nightmare. Best guess at the time before anyone arrived? Probably at least 45 minutes to an hour, even by helicopter. There was a nearby military training base not far from his hacienda. Possible problem, but not probable. The entire central Peru army/security forces and police would be on alert and in rescue and recovery mode. So the question was, what to do? Get the hell out of Ancón was the answer that flashed into his brain.

He retrieved his iPhone from his pocket and dialed his pilot. It rang and rang. No answer. He tried his alternate pilot, same thing. Was he even getting a signal? Perhaps the cell towers had been damaged. He gazed at his phone. All five bars were showing. The simple truth he rapidly came to was there was a lot of damage in Lima, and perhaps he was stuck. Driving would be impossible, it was too far. Flying?

Bernardo had never actually flown the Gulfstream, but he had sat in the co-pilot's seat many times and had it pretty well memorized. It would be possible—maybe. He went inside to look on his computer, pulled up Google Earth, and looked for a landing strip somewhere in the Ica area. Not much. There was one rather long road/strip that seemed to lead to a hangar. The pictures were a little sketchy. He made note of the latitude and longitude coordinates for the south end of the strip. Theoretically, he could punch in the coordinates to the Garmin GPS on board and it would take him to that exact location. Theoretically. Of course there was the issue of filing a flight plan, landing, and other matters. He thought to himself this was an insane idea; on the other hand, an even more insane idea was forming in his brain. Somehow this meeting, these men, had to be stopped at all costs. He knew what GMBI was up to. It was like a scene from that American *Godfather* movie where the people came to ask favors of the Don, in exchange for a "little favor in the future" in return. But first GMBI must ask the blessing of Los Cóndores de Oro. Then, with an ample "tribute" to the group, GMBI could begin to control the food supply of Peru. The hair on the back of Bernardo's head tingled. He thought of Emelia, all her work; was it in vain?

Bernardo left his computer on and went down into the cellar to a small room off to the left of the stairway. The door, although small, was made of reinforced steel, with large rivets all the way around the perimeter. It would be virtually impossible to break it down without heavy equipment. He remembered the day it was installed long ago. A crane had to lower it into place before the upper floors of the hacienda were built. He put his eye up to the biometric scanner, held very still, and then heard a series of bolts sliding into the wall from within the door. The heavy door swung open as if it weighed a pound. He flipped on the light switch on the right and watched as fluorescent light after fluorescent light lit up the darkness as he entered the closet. The "closet" was really more like a long, rectangular armory, with every conceivable weapon neatly lining each wall. There were scores of automatic rifles of every caliber imaginable, and pistols both old school and new. Further to the right were ammunition, grenades, grenade launchers, boxes marked Semtex and C-4, fuses, blasting caps, dynamite, and a few shoulder-launch missiles. It was a virtual arsenal. Bernardo wondered to himself why he had ever collected all this ordinance. Emelia had never approved, and told him he was "totally paranoid," which he always partially agreed with; that is, until now.

He walked down the hallway of death until he got to the Semtex boxes. He opened one and extracted two palm-sized red bricks. The "beauty" of Semtex was its malleability. It could be shaped into nearly anything or any form, and still deliver extremely lethal results with a small detonator or cell phone detonating device. This was the explosive of choice by professional terrorists. It was, fortunately, very expensive, and thus very difficult to come by. However, it could be accomplished with enough money and influence.

Bernardo put a block in each pocket, grabbed a cellular detonator, and switched off the lights and shut the door. A few more items to gather upstairs and down in the tombs of the Inca stronghold, and he would be on his way to Ica.

First, he made a call to his co-conspirator, Angel Gamarra, and let him know he would be arriving in Ica within a day, and staying at the Hotel Las Dunas. Angel expressed surprise that he was coming, in view of what the general had told him, but was "delighted." *I'll bet,* Bernardo thought to himself. No, there was little damage that he was aware of from the terremoto. After hanging up the phone, he spoke briefly to the remaining housekeeper and told her to follow his instructions to the letter in two days' time. He slipped an envelope into her hand, and told her this was a matter of utmost importance. She nodded her head in understanding.

"Si, Patron."

She carried his bags to the car outside, closed the trunk and waved good-bye. *Yes, good-bye indeed,* Bernardo thought to himself grimly. His hands gripped the steering wheel until his knuckles turned white. *Emelia, my darling, I'll see you soon,* he thought to himself, and suddenly relaxed, started the engine, and slowly left the hacienda.

Chapter Twenty-One - Ica

Bernardo drove the Mercedes at an even pace to Santa Rosa; his mind was going in a thousand directions. Beside him, in the passenger seat, were three large brown envelopes, sealed, and addressed to the Minister of Agriculture in Lima, the Editor-in-Chief of *El Comercio*, one of the oldest and most respected newspapers in Lima, and the CNN International office in Lima. Inside each was a short note, explaining the contents (most of the more important of Emelia's seeds, portions of her notebook, and details of why a certain devastating explosion took place in Ica). He had left specific instructions with Julia, the sole remaining housekeeper, to send someone in three days' time to find the envelopes, and to mail them. The 200 soles he gave her made it a sure thing.

He was also listening to the radio as he drove. Stories of death and destruction were starting to come out of Lima. Part of the old Presidential Palace had even collapsed.

Warnings of aftershocks and instructions to locations of National Emergency Centers were repeated over and over again. Citizens were encouraged not to use their cell phones and to stay outdoors so that anticipated aftershocks might not injure any others. Bernardo shut off the radio. He wondered absently if the collapsed palace had any effect on his "good friend" General de la Hoya.

He reached the old racetrack, which was completely deserted, and drove to the far end, where the makeshift hangar covered his Gulfstream. Parking the car next to it, he got out and went to open the trunk. Inside was a suitcase, worn from many years of travel, and a leather briefcase, also worn on the corners. He grabbed the handles, removed the cases and shut the trunk, leaving the car unlocked. Then he climbed the small gangway to the door of the aircraft. He turned the handle, and door silently opened and slid to one side.

Quiet. Six empty seats in the cabin, and two in the cockpit. *I wonder where I should put a briefcase full of Semtex?* he thought to himself. If it blew, would it really matter? He laughed to himself. The insanity of what he was about to do settled in on him. "OK, so I'm going to fly a plane—no, a jet—to a location with no tower or lights, land on a long road, and if I somehow survive, get a ride into town, and two days later, get through ridiculous security, and blow up the most notorious cartel in South America." *No problemo*, he thought to himself with a slight laugh. He dropped his suitcase on the left front seat and fastened a seat belt around it, and then did the same with the Semtex briefcase on the right front seat, securing the belt a little more tightly. "You stay there," he said to the briefcase as he patted the worn, brown leather.

Climbing into the small cockpit, he sat in the pilot seat and stared at the array of dials, displays, and readouts, all of course, blank. He put the headphones on, although he couldn't imagine what he would need them for, and leaned down to switch the batteries on. Immediately, lights began to come alive across the whole front and top of the cockpit. Readouts were beginning to spit out numbers, most of which were meaningless to him. Bernardo did know where the start engine buttons were, and he initiated startup of number one, and then number two, listening as they began to whine as they spun up.

Interior lighting came on, and he checked to see that the parking brake was set. It was still early afternoon so he reached up and set the strobe on, leaving the landing and taxi lights off. He looked down at the display for gas. Nearly three-quarters full. Theoretically this was going to be a short hop, and he would be flying at relatively low altitudes, so he should have no problems with fuel. The radio was set for the last contact they had made before landing in Santa Rosa.

He eased the flaps back until they read 20 degrees. He looked at the Garmin, and set the navigation to fly on GPS rules, manually entering the latitude and longitude coordinates on the tiny keyboard for the destination. A full color map came up on the screen with a line from Santa Rosa to just outside of Ica, reading estimated distance 393 km, ETA approximately one hour at 199.86 knots.

Bernardo looked at the autopilot and set the cruising altitude for 4,500 feet, the heading for 145 degrees (slightly southeast), and the speed for 200 knots. Once he got into the air—IF he got into the air—he would hit the master control on the autopilot, and the rest would pretty much be taken care of between autopilot and the GPS. Of course, there was that little issue of landing….

Bernardo took a deep breath, released the parking brake, and grabbed the yoke. The jet began to move ever so slightly out of the hangar towards the blacktop. He turned slowly towards the right to taxi to the end of the road just before the turn. As he applied the brakes, the plane jerked to a stop. So sensitive! He had very little room to turn, so he released the left brake, and gently increased the throttle on the right engine momentarily, then throttled it back to idle. It was enough to gently spin the plane around and face the length of the track. He centered the plane, locked the steering, and put on the brakes again, more gently this time.

"God help me," he whispered, crossing himself.

He released the brakes, pulled the throttles all the way back, and was immediately shoved back into his chair by the thrust of the twin engines. He studied the speed and the runway. The speed rapidly inched towards 100...120...130...150. He looked up and noticed he was also rapidly running out of asphalt. He pulled back on the yoke. The plane lifted gracefully into the air. Altitude: 30 meters...75 meters...100 meters...210 meters...250 meters. He glanced at the speed. Way too fast, approaching 400 knots. Alarms were going off, adding to his rising panic. He had forgotten about the autopilot. He reached for the master control and pushed it on. The engines began to slow down, and he watched the throttles ease back towards him as the plane began a sharp bank toward the southeast. Flaps! He pulled the flaps forward to zero. The plane sped up, but still felt sluggish. *Mierda!* he thought to himself, and reached forward to retract the landing gear into the fuselage until the lights on the panel all clicked from green to red.

The aircraft leveled off from its bank, reading a perfect 145, and continued its ascent to 4,500 feet.

He sat back in his seat with relief. It was only then that he realized he had never strapped himself into the pilot's harness, the harness that might very well keep him alive if he ever made it to his destination. Sweat ran down his forehead and burned into his eyes. He wiped his face with the back of his hand. Part one accomplished. He gazed at the GPS map, and noted that his aircraft was following a perfect line to his destination. He was jolted out of his slight relaxation by a loud voice in his headphones,

"Unknown aircraft this is Lima flight control. Repeat this is Lima flight control. Please identify yourself. What is your aircraft, altitude, heading destination and squawk code?"

Bernardo had heard the chatter from the pilots enough to possibly fake his way through this. He clicked the radio, "Roger Lima Control, this is Gulfstream Oscar Bravo Romeo, niner four one, squawk 6501 currently at 45 zero zero, heading one four five, copy?"

"Roger Gulfstream Oscar Bravo Romeo niner four one, altitude is four niner zero, you're too low. Please recalibrate and climb to 6,500. Copy?

Another stupid mistake. His altimeter was set for nearly sea level, not the mountainous territory he was flying over now.

This was one of the most basic of all checklist requirements for flight.

"Uhh, roger Lima Control, altitude four niner zero, climb to six five zero zero." This awkward turn of events had probably prevented Bernardo from flying into the side of a mountain. He reached over and set the altitude on the autopilot to 6,500 and the plane began to lift up.

"Gulfstream Oscar Bravo Romeo niner four one, what is your destination please?"

He couldn't tell them Ica—there was no landing field in Ica. The only way in was a four-hour drive on the Pan-American from Lima. According to his GPS, the closest possible airport was Coronel FAP Alfredo Mendívil Duarte Airport in Ayacucho.

"Lima Control, this is Gulfstream Oscar Bravo Romeo niner four one, destination is Alpha Yankee Papa in Ayacucho."

"Roger Gulfstream Oscar Bravo Romeo niner four one, please tune to Pisco Control at one five niner point three zero."

"Roger Lima Control, tuning to one five niner point three zero," said Bernardo, and reached over and shut off the radio. After a second thought, he shut off the transponder, too. He prayed silently that he would have enough time to get to his destination before Lima Control scrambled some F-14 Tomcats to check him out.

He was about seventy miles out from his destination. Flying in was going to be all visual. There were no ILS instrument controls to glide-slope him in, and he knew he would only get one shot at it. It was a huge, if not insane gamble. He looked out over the expanse of brown, mountainous terrain below and around him. How the hell was he going to find this place? Forty miles to destination.

He had to start a slow descent and also cut his speed. He reached over to the autopilot and made the necessary adjustments. As the plane began to descend, it began to pick up speed, even though he was lowering the speed of his engines. Flaps! He put the flaps to 15 degrees. Immediately the plane slowed down to less than 200, then 190. His altitude had descended to the 3,000 feet he had set on the autopilot. He reset his GPS for closer magnification. There on the GPS was a long, straight line that must be the road. He squinted out into the distance. He saw it, coming up fast. He was way too high and going way too fast. His gut tightened up. He was going to have to land this flying bomb manually. He reached forward and cut off the autopilot master control. Everything went to manual immediately, and the plane began to drift.

Reaching to the throttle panel he pulled back slightly, hearing the engines beginning to wind down, and pushed the yoke forward. Speed 160, Altitude 2,500. He was veering off to the right. He corrected by turning the yoke to the left, but overcorrected and was now too far to the left. Speed 120, altitude 1,000.

His GPS indicated he was at his destination. How the hell did people fly these things? He was just about in a panic. Oh shit, the landing...! He pushed the gear handle down. After what seemed to be an indefinite time, red lights turned to green on all three gears, and he heard them lock into place. He corrected slightly again to the right. The plane was dragging more with the gear down. He could see the long road straight ahead of him, but it seemed too high.

In desperation, he pulled the flaps to 100 percent, pulled the engines to idle, and pulled back on the yoke to flare up on landing. Too much. The nose rose way up in the air and a stall alarm sounded. "Pull up, pull up!" the goddamn plane was talking—no, yelling at him! He pushed the yoke a little more down. He could see the ground and the road. The alarm stopped.

Suddenly the Gulfstream hit the ground and bounced into the air again. He pushed the nose down and flared again, this time with less enthusiasm, and the front end came down. The plane was bouncing hard on the broken asphalt road. He wondered if he would lose a landing gear. Speed was still 80 mph. He pulled back on the engine throttle to reverse thrust and began to stand on the brakes. The aircraft slowed down and skidded to the left and then to the right as he corrected. He put the engines to idle and smelled burning rubber, finally coming to a stop just 20 meters from the end of the road. He leaned over to his right, switched off the engines, and vomited onto the co-pilot's seat.

CHAPTER TWENTY-TWO

Bernardo opened the main hatch, folded out the stairs to the ground, and staggered out of the aircraft into the cool evening air. The desert cooled down rapidly as the sun set in these areas; nothing to hold the heat. He took some deep breaths and tried to slow his pounding heart, scanning the surroundings for lights or movement, but there was none. At the end of the road he saw a series of abandoned chicken farmhouses, which, true, from Google Earth looked like a possible hangar, but wasn't. So much for hiding the aircraft. It was totally silent around him. He opened the front cargo hold where luggage was normally stored. What appeared to be a neatly folded series of pipes, when pulled out and assembled, became a remarkably light, small, portable electric moped, made almost completely out of carbon fiber material. He strapped his small grip and briefcase onto the back with a bungee cord, turned on the GPS on his phone, turned the ignition to "on," and quietly slipped into the night, heading for Ica.

With a great deal of trouble, he navigated the back dirt roads until he found the scattered lights of the Pan-American Highway, and followed it silently into Ica, turning onto the Avenue La Angostura and arriving at his destination, Hotel Las Dunas. It was not unusual to see people coming and going in and on all manners of transportation. Dune buggies and other four-wheelers abounded due to one of the local sports here, riding up and down the sand dunes that surrounded the area.

Bernardo parked his moped alongside the hotel with other bicycles, turned off the engine, and locked the moped to the bicycle rack. No matter if it was stolen, it had served its purpose. He removed his briefcase and grip and proceeded to the front of the hotel. Refusing assistance, he checked into the hotel and went directly to his room. It was spacious; a large king-size bed, a sitting room, fully stocked kitchen, two bathrooms, and a magnificent view of the lagoon that the hotel was built around. Tasteful artwork was scattered on the brightly colored walls, with an assortment of familiar Nazca images and weavings casually draped on leather furniture.

Bernardo retrieved some Perrier from the small refrigerator and sat down. This had been a harrowing day...and tomorrow? Tomorrow was going to take some planning. He opened his briefcase and removed the two small red blocks of Semtex. One of the features of most Semtex was the presence of a substance called DMNB, chemically 2,3 Dimethyl-2,3 Dinitro Butane, which was mixed into the nearly odorless explosive deliberately to be detected by dogs or other vapor detection electronics. Bernardo's Semtex had bypassed that process in a "specially manufactured lot," which cost an enormous sum of money. He now thanked himself for doing the research so long ago. Once again, his meticulous attention to detail had paid off.

Removing the inner silk and leather lining of the top of his briefcase, Bernardo gently unwrapped the outer covering of the Semtex. Slowly, he massaged it into a flatter and flatter shape, fitting it into the back, until it fit exactly into the top of the briefcase. He took a glass from the table and rolled it across the surface until it was universally smooth and thin. He replaced the lining over the Semtex and examined his handiwork. It would be very difficult, if not impossible to notice, especially after he replaced the leather folders and pockets and filled them with the papers, pens, and other contraptions used in the twenty-first century to do modern business. The amount of explosive in this briefcase was now capable of removing half an entire city block. Removing a tiny wire from a calculator, he placed it through the silk lining, and very gently into the high explosive. The calculator (it actually worked) was also a very simple one-way cellular device, capable of receiving calls, and then detonating itself with enough force to trigger the Semtex.

Bernardo paused to wipe the back of his right hand over his forehead. He noticed his hand was shaking slightly. Part one, accomplished. He needed to make contact with Angel and find out exactly where the meeting was going to occur. In the past, these details were usually left until the last moment to avoid attention and keep security high. He was sure it would not be in town, so he was in need of a car. He called the concierge on the house phone.

"This is Señor Villacorta. I'll need a car and a driver tomorrow morning, preferably Juan. Have him here early, around seven. Make arrangements to have Juan and the car available to me all day, please." Bernardo had used this company, and Juan, many times. They were very discreet and security conscious.

The concierge informed him that the car would be ready in front of the hotel at 7:00 a.m. sharp.

Bernardo reached into his pocket, retrieved his cell phone, and turned it on. He had deliberately left it off since he'd left the hacienda in Ancón so he couldn't be tracked. He noticed seven voice mails waiting for him just as he was about to speed-dial Angel Gamarra. He pressed the voice mail button. The first, second, and third messages were all from the same number, a number in Lima which he did not recognize. Apparently someone really wanted to talk to him.

First message: "Señor Villacorta, this is Lieutenant Perez, the general's assistant." His voice sounded out of breath and tense. "Señor, the terremoto, it caused very serious damage in parts of the palace. The general...señor, the general is dead." Bernardo felt as if he had been punched directly in the solar plexus. It was as if all the air had left the room.

Second message: "Señor, please call this number as soon as possible. I have been instructed to give you important information." The call ended.

Third message: "Señor Villacorta. This is Lieutenant Perez. Please call as soon as possible." The line went dead again.

This changed everything. His brain was going in a million directions. *Will the meeting still occur? Maybe I should re-think this whole thing. I definitely need to get rid of the plane now.* Bernardo had pretty much resigned himself to dying with the others, or being caught and killed. Either way, he figured the Gulfstream wouldn't be important. Now, perhaps it would.

He reached for his phone and called his most trusted pilot, Geraldo. The answer was immediate.

"Hello, Señor Villacorta. How may I be of service?"

"Buenas noches, Geraldo. I have an important assignment for you, and it must be done with the utmost discretion; do you understand?"

"Si, señor, anything." Geraldo knew that there would be a lot of money in whatever his boss was about to tell him.

"Geraldo, I'm currently in Ica. I know you probably find this hard to believe, but I actually flew the Gulfstream here by myself."

"Are you serious?" he blurted out, forgetting for a moment who he was talking to. "I mean, señor, without any help? I don't remember any airports in Ica. Where exactly did you land?"

"That's exactly it, Geraldo, there was no landing strip. I somehow managed to put it down on a long dirt and asphalt road outside of Ica. Before you ask, the aircraft was not damaged."

"That's truly amazing, señor," he said, with a bit of skepticism in his voice. "Anyway, how may I assist you?"

"Where are you now?" Bernardo asked.

"I'm with my family in Lima, señor."

"Good. Here's what I would like you to do; and I assume you know you will be well-rewarded for this. Get a paper and pen and write down these coordinates. You'll also need a GPS. Your cell phone may do, although the reception in this particular spot may not be that good." He heard shuffling in the background while the pilot scrambled to find paper and pen.

"Ready, señor."

Bernardo read him the exact coordinates where the plane was sitting. He only hoped it was still there. It wasn't exactly the most unobtrusive object in a sea of brown sand.

"Someone is obviously going to have to take you there, Geraldo. Be absolutely sure you can trust that person..." he paused for effect, "with your life. It could come down to that, if things go sideways. Also, bring a can of compressed air to blow out the turbines. They've been exposed to desert sand, and I wouldn't know what's blown in there in the 24 hours it will have been in its current placement. File a flight plan once you're at altitude. Take the plane directly to Jose Prado to our hangar, lock it up, and leave. Can you do this, Geraldo?" he asked firmly.

"Si, si señor, I'll leave immediately. I know my brother will drive me there. He can be absolutely trusted."

"Good, Geraldo. Did the earthquake affect you? Is your family all right?"

"Oh, we were a little shook up, but no damage, señor. A few broken dishes, nothing serious. But there are still aftershocks. It's making travel difficult, but we will find a way out."

"Good. Please take care of this as soon as you can get away. Call me immediately when you land in Lima, and I'll wire 56,000 soles into your account for your trouble. Any questions?"

"No, señor. I'll call you tomorrow when we return. Gracias." The line went dead.

Bernardo knew that Geraldo was an expert pilot and would be exceptionally discreet, saying as little to his brother as was necessary. He said a silent prayer to himself, hoping that the aircraft could be returned without incident.

What's next? he wondered to himself. *Call Angel.*

CHAPTER TWENTY-THREE

Bernardo glanced at his watch. It was already 11: 35. He considered whether to call Angel or not. On the one hand it would appear suspicious if he didn't know where and when the meeting was tomorrow. But on the other, he wanted to weigh the conversation of not knowing about Victor's rather sudden demise, against the consequences for tomorrow if he just played stupid.

Bernardo had never been a very good liar. He had compensated for that by mastering the art of silence, both in business dealings, and in conversation. He had learned that in saying nothing, and leaving a period of silence for even as little as ten seconds, it made whomever he was speaking with uncomfortable. It inevitably pushed the person he was talking to, to say more, hopefully to supply more information to fill the conversational void the silence created in the first place. The longer the silence, the more power he gained. It was a simple but very effective tool of allowing people to expose themselves through anxiety. He decided to call and say nothing when Angel told him about Victor, and see what would be revealed.

He took out his cell phone and pushed the speed-dial button for Angel Gamarra in his contacts. After three rings, a voice answered that did not sound like the Angel he was used to talking with.

"Angel, this is Bernardo. How are you?" He paused.

"Bernardo. Are you here in town? Where are you staying? Have you heard about Victor?"

The questions came so quickly, he hardly had a chance to answer one before the next.

"Angel, you seem very upset, are you all right?" he replied, taking the offence.

"Bernardo, I know you have been in Cuzco for a while. Are you not aware of the terremoto in Lima?"

"The clerk mentioned something about it when I got in late this afternoon. I've been so busy preparing for the meeting

I haven't turned on the news. Was it bad?" He waited and counted seconds: 1...2...3...4...5...6....

"Bad? Bad? Bernardo, Victor is dead! His offices in the palace were destroyed. He must have fallen during the quake and hit his head. We're all very shaken by this. Are you telling me you didn't know?"

Bernardo waited again before speaking. 1...2...3...4...5... he counted all the way to 15 seconds before Angel couldn't take it.

"Bernardo, are you there? Hello?"

"Yes, yes Angel, I'm here. I'm just stunned by your news. I'm not sure what to say. This is devastating. Victor? We have known each other for so long...." He strained to sound brokenhearted in the way he spoke.

More silence, and then he spoke.

"So, what are we going to do? I assume there will be services. Are we all going back to Lima? Is this postponing our meeting?"

"No. We will meet tomorrow as scheduled, and then we will discuss how to proceed with Victor's funeral. We were all in agreement, although the circumstances are tragic. We felt the meeting is so important, and many people have come from so far away, not to mention the GMBI people, that we should continue. Victor would have wanted that, I'm sure."

"Why wasn't I consulted about this, Angel?" Bernardo left the question hanging in the air.

"We tried to reach you on your phone, but it went directly to voice mail, Bernardo. You must have been in a bad spot, or the terremoto took out a tower, or something. I personally left three separate messages. Have you not listened to them?"

Bernardo remembered there had been several voice mails on his phone. He had only listed to the first three from the lieutenant.

"No, Angel, my phone…ahhh, you know these damned things. Something is always a problem. So, I understand; and I confess, I agree with your decision. So, where will we be meeting, and when?" and then threw in, "I just can't believe what you're telling me…it can't be possible." He sniffled a little for good measure.

"Tomorrow morning, probably all day. Is your phone working well enough to receive texts? I can send you the location."

"Yes, I believe it is now. It seems to be working fine now. Send me the information. If I don't receive it, I'll call you back."

"All right, Bernardo. I'll text you the pin on the map. Just follow the route. It's out of town, a small hacienda that has been graciously donated to us for the meeting. You'll see the cars. We plan on starting at nine. Are you all right with that?"

"Si, si, that will be fine. All right, Angel, I'll see you in the morning then. I...I really haven't taken in this horrible news about Victor yet. I feel numb. I must go now. I'll see you tomorrow, Angel. Send me the location now before we hang up."

"OK," said Angel, "I'm sending it now."

Bernardo's phone made a sound, and miraculously, a map with a red pin appeared on his phone.

"Got it." Bernardo wanted to get off the phone. "All right, Angel, until tomorrow," he said, and hung up.

Bernardo flopped backwards on his oversized king bed and sighed. *OK, now I know time, place, and cast of characters... what to do?* There was this ticking time bomb in the back of his mind that was going to go off, with or without his current plans, when his housekeeper sent those envelopes he had left behind in Ancón. He was either going to look like a complete fool, or complete the circle of villainy that had plagued him for the past few weeks. He needed to sleep, but realized it would be next to impossible.

CHAPTER TWENTY-FOUR

Bernardo rose early. He had hardly slept at all. He glanced at the clock on the bedside table: 5:48 a.m. He decided to shower, shave, and get ready to be downstairs for the driver at 7:00 a.m. He had determined that it would be better if he paid the driver to leave the car with him after he was dropped off at the hacienda. Depending on how things evolved, by around 1:00 p.m. he would either be dead, severely wounded, or in need of a car to make a rapid departure. He also knew the driver would be suspicious, and would require a large sum of money to leave the car with him all day. He would make up a story about needing to see a lover, not know when they would be done, and he would return the car in pristine condition that evening (God willing).

After dressing, Bernardo grabbed his briefcase, opened it, and activated the cellular calculator detonator by pressing the Fn button and then 8797. He closed the briefcase, put the hotel key in his pocket, and left for the lobby. It was 6:39 a.m.

True to form, Juan, in his formal black suit, was waiting in the lobby, reading a newspaper. He was always early, never late.

"Juan!" Bernardo called out to him as he approached the stocky driver.

Juan quickly folded the paper and rose to his feet. "Señor! How are you? I wasn't expecting you until at least seven."

"Oh, you know...strange hotels," he said. "You can never sleep well on a strange bed." He started moving towards the front doors. "Shall we go?" he said, hoping he wasn't sounding too anxious.

"Of course, señor," Juan said, and hurriedly went to open the door for Bernardo, and led him to the black Mercedes parked in front of the hotel. It was just daybreak, with a misty chill in the air. The sun rose over the desert to the east, cutting through the slight gray that surrounded them, revealing dark, colorless shapes of palm trees and flowers.

Juan opened the rear door on the passenger side for Bernardo to get in. Once he was safely inside, Juan closed the car door and scurried around to the driver's seat, fastened his belt and said, "So. Where to?"

"I'll direct you, Juan. Just head out west on this road out front. It will be a hacienda, perhaps eighty-five kilometers from here. Take your time; we will no doubt be early." Bernardo had pulled out his phone and was following the route that had been mapped out from the hotel to the pin Angel had sent him.

"Si, señor," Juan replied, and accelerated out of the hotel grounds, heading west.

They travelled for about fifteen minutes before Bernardo decided to casually mention the car.

"Juan, we have known each other for many years, yes?"

"Si. Si, Patron, we have."

"And you know I'm a man of my word."

"Oh, yes, Patron. Of course you are."

"Good. Juan, I must ask you a favor, but it will require the utmost discretion on your part. Know that you will be handsomely compensated if you give me the correct answer..." he let the last part hang in the air. He had Juan's interest immediately. He could see Juan's eyes looking at him through the rearview mirror.

"Of course, Patron. Whatever you need, would like, I'm at your disposal. There is no need for concern, señor. I don't even know we're having this conversation," he said, with a slight smile on his face.

"Very well. I'll need the use of your car for the rest of the day once we get to our destination, but without you. I have to visit someone, a young lady, later in the afternoon, and I would require that you not be present or have to wait for me. Do you understand?"

"Si, Patron. I understand."

"I'll call a cab for you and have you returned to wherever you want. I'll also return your car this evening, no later than 10:00 p.m., in front of the hotel. Do you have another set of keys?"

"Si, señor, I do.

"Good, then I'll lock this set in the glove box for you. I'll also give you 10,000 soles for your trouble. Will that be acceptable?"

Juan's head was spinning. He would not make that much money in three months. "Si. Si, Patron. That would be very generous of you, and will not be a problem."

"Good. Thank you, Juan. It's settled then. I'll call a cab for you when we arrive. You can just leave the keys with me." Bernardo relaxed in the back seat and checked off another item on his list for the morning. He looked at his watch. It was 7:58 a.m.

As they neared the hacienda, there were security men at the entrance to the driveway. After passing the questioning of the first two guards and a large German shepherd, the car was checked from one end to the other, with mirrors being used under the car. They were then greeted further up the driveway by three more men, all in suits, brandishing machine guns. They looked very serious. Juan pulled up slowly to the guard on his side of the car. The guard looked into the car.

"Name, señor?" and pulled out a piece of paper from the inside pocket of his jacket.

"Bernardo Villacorta." Bernardo made a point of looking right into the man's eyes. The man glanced at the list. He nodded to the other guards, and whispered something into a radio that was attached to his lapel.

"Thank you," he said to Juan. "You may proceed to the main house."

Juan drove forward up the driveway and stopped near the front entrance of the large house. It was brick, and covered with vines. All around were carefully tended flower gardens, with groups of different colors of bougainvillea draping the front entrance. Men were out front smoking, mostly drivers, but some Bernardo recognized. Juan was opening the door for Bernardo as he caught the glance of Angel Gamarra, who waved to him as he got out of the car.

"I'll explain to the head of security that you're leaving your car with me, Juan. Wait here. I'll signal you when to go. There will be a cab waiting for you at the entrance in about an hour." Bernardo walked briskly towards the group.

"Señor!" he heard Juan's voice call from behind him. He turned to look over his shoulder. Juan was discreetly waving the keys in his hand near his pocket.

"Ah, yes!" Bernardo said, returning to the car. He took the keys from Juan and quickly put them in his pocket.

"Thank you, Juan. I'm not thinking clearly yet." Juan simply smiled and waited by the car.

Bernardo strode back up the driveway towards the crowd of men. Angel was first to greet him.

"Bernardo!" he exclaimed, with perhaps a bit too much exuberance, Bernardo thought. It wasn't like they were that great of friends. He decided to return with the same tone.

"Angel! My old friend, how good to see you. What a beautiful place for a meeting; and the weather...it just couldn't be better, eh?" *Puke,* he thought to himself. That was so unlike his style of being with friends.

Angel came forward, put his arm around Bernardo's shoulders and said, "Come, let's go inside and get some food. You must be starving."

Bernardo wondered how he had known he hadn't eaten breakfast. He decided to test his theory.

"Oh, no, Angel, I had a huge breakfast at the hotel. I'm really not that hungry, but coffee would be good."

Angel hesitated for just the briefest of moments, and then reacted, confirming Bernardo's suspicion.

"Oh. Well then, of course…" he hesitated. "If you've already eaten…well then, you can watch me!" and he laughed almost too hard. Was he being watched?

They walked together into the spacious entranceway. Beautiful artwork was displayed on all the walls, large chandeliers hung from several areas of the grand hallway, and worn but beautiful oriental rugs covered the old wooden floors. A large circular stairway led up to the second floor. Men were coming in and out of a large room to the left with food and drinks. The noise level increased dramatically. Men were talking loudly, laughing, and saying hello to each other. These meetings were not on any regular basis, and usually involved very serious matters. Better to eat and laugh now before "Business" began.

Bernardo glanced at his watch; 8:47 a.m. The meeting would start promptly at 9:00 a.m. He made an excuse to use the bathroom, and made his way to the back of the house. He saw a guard, and asked to speak with the head of security.

"He is outside, señor. I can get him to come in by radio if you like."

"No," Bernardo said, "that won't be necessary. Can you please ask him if it's all right if my driver returns to the road to wait for a cab? His wife has fallen ill and he needs to get back to Ica. I have already arranged for a cab to have him picked up at the road. I'll keep his car and return it to the hotel this evening."

"Certainly, señor," said the guard, and whispered into his microphone. After a few moments, he held his hand to his earpiece and said, "Everything is cleared for your driver to leave, señor. What is his name?"

Bernardo told him. He thanked the guard for his trouble, and made his way to the bathroom. Good, he had a cell phone signal. He called the pre-entered number for the cab company to make the arrangements, and checked off another item on his mental checklist.

As he came out of the bathroom, he heard the crowd noise even louder, and noticed a line of men going up the stairs. He got in line and followed up the grand staircase, where the line turned to the right and went down a long hallway, ending in a large room, perhaps once a ballroom. There was a huge oval table set with tablets, pens, papers, and in the middle, perhaps every five feet, there were silver trays filled with drinks, bottled water, and bowls of fruit and candies. As he entered the room, he saw there were cards in front of each large, comfortable leather chair with names on them. Men were walking around the table to find their place, as did Bernardo. He found his; unfortunately, it was fairly far from the doorway. Victor de la Hoya (empty) on his left, and Ricardo Pariguana to his right. He did not know him. He did know the Pariguana name from the Cuzco area, however, and wondered if he was from there. He would have to ask.

He took his seat at the table as others entered the room, scanned for their places, and took seats. Bernardo took his briefcase and placed it on the table next to him. He opened the case and prepared mentally for his next move. He had planned to wait until discussions were well under way. Once talks of finance ensued, he would have an excuse to pull out his "calculator," punch in the code to activate the detonator, and find a reason to use the bathroom.

A large screen hung from the ceiling on the south end of the table, and a projector was connected to a laptop near the front of the area, where none other than Sr. Luis Castellano himself was the presenter from GMBI. At the opposite end of the table sat the acting director, Juan Miguel Tapia Rebolledo, a very large Peruvian man from the Ica district. Eating well apparently was one of his weaknesses.

The cartel was divided into districts, more to know who was from where than to designate a territory that was controlled by them. He looked around the room at the 47 faces and thought to himself, as he had so many times before, *The accumulated wealth and power in this room is frightening. The people, the real, everyday people who work in their offices, toil in the fields, or run their little puppet governments have no idea, no idea what is really happening!* It reminded him of that American movie he had seen on a plane once, *The Matrix*, where nothing was what it appeared to be. And in this room today, control of the entire continent's food supply was about to be determined. Perhaps. Bernardo smiled to himself, and sat back in his chair.

"Gentlemen!" a loud voice at the far end of the table boomed. The room became silent almost instantly.

"Gentlemen, welcome to all of you, and thank you for coming to meet on such an occasion as this!" said Sr. Rebolledo as he stood up. "As you know, we have been involved in talks with our friends from GMBI," motioning with his right arm towards the other end of the table, "...who have come today to make an important offer to each of us, which I think we all agree, will make us some serious money!" he said, laughing. As if on cue, everyone else laughed, as if a sign of acceptance. Bernardo smiled, but did not laugh. *What the hell would we possibly need any more money for?* he thought to himself. *Each one of these men could own whatever they wanted right now...* He stared at his briefcase and swallowed hard. And one or more of these vipers had killed his wife and several of his friends to get to this point. Heat burned in his heart. He was ready now. He had nothing but contempt for the cartel at this point. He tried to keep his face cheerful and look interested.

"As you all know," boomed Sr. Rebolledo, "our comrade, General Victor de la Hoya, was tragically killed just yesterday in Lima during the earthquake. I would like to honor his memory with a moment of silence please."

The room fell especially silent, with many pairs of eyes shifting to the empty seat next to him. Bernardo closed his eyes and said a silent prayer. *And may your avenging angels bring down death and destruction to the rest of these jackals...* he thought to himself.

"Thank you. Thank you all. However, we must move on. Today, we have the honor of listening to a presentation from Sr. Luis Castellano, Executive Vice President for Research and Development for GMBI. Won't you please welcome him?" He waved to the far end of the table as Luis got to his feet.

Loud applause erupted from the members, and polite attention was given to the man now standing at the far end of the room. He held a remote control. With a quick click, the screen displayed the GMBI corporate logo, and Sr. Luis Castellano began what would be the last presentation of his fairly short life.

CHAPTER TWENTY-FIVE - THE CALL

The presentation was quite dazzling. There were charts, graphs, and spreadsheets in full color, showing details of crops, locations, coverage, yield projections going out five years, net profits that were staggering to the imagination, and the one solitary and extremely significant piece of information that was revealed in all its naked, unabashed glory: total control of the continent's food! The presentation revealed the research that Emelia had been doing herself (not naming her, of course), and had taken it to the next level; a seed that could not be used again—a sterile grain that was native corn or soybean, or wheat, or barley, or rye grass, or quinoa. All reduced to a patented commodity that could not be reproduced without growers purchasing the seed for crops the following year.

As an added bonus, the yield was so high that the crop required larger and larger amounts of land to fuel the greed of the growers, and larger, more expensive machinery to harvest the crops. The growers went into debt to buy the equipment, conveniently provided by GMBI Finance at astronomical interest rates. Growers could barely afford the new seed to keep things going for the next year and make interest payments on their giant equipment. To make any profit, the growers had to hold back yield to keep market costs up, which necessitated storage bins. Huge storage bins, and additional cost to the grower. Seed costs were directly proportional to GMBI's "contract fees," which were in direct proportion to whatever the cartel decided. The world's largest scam ever. He thought of a quote from Henry Kissinger, the former Secretary of State in the United States that he had read long ago: "If you control the food supply, you control the people." He shuddered unconsciously. And as a codicil, if you control the growers, then you truly control the entire food chain.

It was time to excuse himself and go to the bathroom. He was feeling slightly nauseated. As the presentation was nearing an end and awaiting questions, Bernardo punched the code into the calculator in his open briefcase, pushed his seat back silently from the table, and excused himself. Two security men opened the doors for him to leave. He muttered something about a bad prostate and caught a smirk from one of the men. He walked to end of the hallway and started to descend the stairs towards the front of the hacienda. About halfway down, a voice from the balcony said, "Excuse me, señor." He kept going down the stairs and glanced over his shoulder.

"Señor!" the voice became a bit more insistent. He stopped his descent. Turning, he saw a security "suit" speaking softly into a radio as he was watching Bernardo.

"Señor, if you don't mind, I must ask you where you're going," he said respectfully.

Bernardo decided that he should exude confidence and slight annoyance to put the guard off balance. After all, he was just doing his job. He felt his heart rate go up slightly.

"Not that it's any of your concern, but I'm going out for a little air. Why? Do you want to come with me?" he said in an irritated tone.

"Señor, I apologize. I must know where everyone is. You of course must know that. There are always security risks..." He left the words echoing slightly in the cavernous lobby.

"Yes, yes, I understand," he snapped back impatiently. And then he gambled. "Come with me if you want, I can use the company!" and Bernardo gestured to the front door.

"No, Patron. I must stay here. I'll notify someone outside that you're coming, but please return quickly," the guard said, wondering what this might cost him if he were questioned later.

"As you wish," chided Bernardo, and silently sighed relief and proceeded towards the front door.

He stepped outside into the sunlight, covering his eyes with one hand and feeling for the detonator phone in his pocket with the other. A guard emerged from a group of men under the shade of some trees and came towards him.

"Señor, is everything all right? May I help you?" asked the well-built security man. His smile belied the significant bulge under the left side of his jacket. *A Beretta, no doubt,* thought Bernardo.

"No, no, I'm fine," he said, still covering his eyes from the sun. "Is there a problem?"

"Patron," said the man haltingly. He measured his words so as not to offend this powerful man standing before him. "It's just that we have been given very strict orders to not let anyone in or out of the facility while all of you are meeting. I'm sorry, señor, but I'll have to ask you to go back inside."

Bernardo thought about the next move. He was so close! He knew he would have to comply, or invite further scrutiny. He needed to buy just a little time. "Of course," he said slowly. "Just a few minutes, please." He took several dramatic deep breaths to emphasize the need for air, waving his hand in front of his face. "It's so stuffy in that room."

The security guard relaxed slightly. "Very well, Patron, just a few minutes. I'll be over here in the shade." He walked back to the small stand of trees where two other men sat with their jackets off, shoulder holsters at the ready, playing cards.

He had just reached into his pocket to press the "1" button on the calculator, which would speed-dial the detonator, when a noise came from his phone in the other pocket. He was startled by its intrusion. He reached into his pocket and retrieved his personal cell. A picture was displayed, along with a name. He stared at the phone in disbelief. He felt his heart simply stop beating. The ringing droned on and on. Looking back at him was his wife. The phone had her name Emelia displayed. Emelia. Emelia?

He began to shake as he pressed the answer button. He felt faint. "Hello?" he said, almost breathless.

"Bernardo, my darling. I know this must come as a shock to you. I don't know where you are, but I do know you must be in danger right now. I'm alive! Try your best to not show any emotion. We will be together soon, I promise. You must get to our hacienda in Ancón as soon as you can. I have spoken with Julia. She showed me one of the envelopes." Silence.

Bernardo heard his voice, but it wasn't the one he was used to. He was weeping. His weeping turned into sobs. He felt overwhelmed with joy, but struggled to speak.

"Emelia….how can…I…my God. Is this possible?" There was still a part of him, even though he knew it was his wife's voice, that thought this had to be someone playing him. A last, final slap in the face. A diversion. Someone had found out. This was impossible. He had seen her….

"Darling, hang up the phone, NOW!" she said. "I'll contact you in two hours. You must get away from wherever you are, quickly. Please, darling, I know you must be beside yourself right now. Listen to me. Hang up. Erase this call from the phone log, and leave. I must go. Good-bye, darling." The phone went silent. He stared at the cell phone. It was as if he was waiting for her to say more. He was having difficulty thinking. He followed her directions and cleared the phone log. Tears were still streaming down his face. How could this be? He felt as if his knees were starting to buckle. He was having a hard time catching his breath. He knew he was going into shock. His blood pressure was dropping.

The security man had witnessed the entire event and was approaching him from the shaded area. The entire last few seconds had taken on a surreal quality. It was as if everything had suddenly gone into slow motion, and he had all the time in the world. He put his cell phone into his pocket, wiped the tears from his eyes with the back of his hand, reached into his other pocket, and as the guard passed forty meters in front of him with his back to the hacienda, he pushed the "1" on his calculator detonator. Two seconds later, the entire area exploded in a fireball that knocked him backwards and unconscious, with the impact of a truck hitting him squarely in the chest, raining down debris in a shower of fire, dust and body parts.

CHAPTER TWENTY-SIX

The remnants of that day were sketchy to Bernardo. He lay in the back of a truck, wounded and partially deaf. Bandages soaked in blackening blood were wrapped around his arms, face and chest. His shirt flapped in the breeze of the truck flatbed as he bounced painfully along the road, some road. It was growing dark. He glanced over to the side of his makeshift bed made of sacks of grain arranged in such a way that it would at least hold him from falling out of the truck. Sitting in a squatting position were two men; one he recognized as Juan, the driver from the morning, and another man. They were dressed in typical farmer clothing; jeans, T-shirts, and long-sleeved flannel shirts and cowboy boots. Juan's flapping flannel shirt revealed a Brazilian FIFA soccer T-shirt underneath. He reached towards Bernardo.

"Señor, it's good to see you awake. We were worried."

"Where…what…" Bernardo struggled to get his thoughts together. It hurt to breathe. The voices seemed to be from very far away.

"You're badly injured, señor. Don't talk now. We're taking you to a doctor we know in the country. We need to get as far away from the explosion as possible. There are people everywhere looking for whoever did this." Juan looked genuinely frightened as he scanned the countryside in the failing light. He began to fill in the blanks for Bernardo as they traversed along the rough road.

Apparently, a terrible explosion had occurred at the hacienda where he had dropped Bernardo off that morning. At first everyone thought it must have been terrorists, or a burst gas pipe from the earthquake, but no one, at least at the present time, seemed to really know. What remained of the building was now a huge smoking crater, debris scattered everywhere. It was a miracle that anyone made it. There was only one survivor, according to the police; a guard whom they did not expect to live. Bernardo's body had been thrown away from the building almost one hundred meters into a pile of brush that must have saved him by breaking his fall. Locals had found him and moved him to a farmhouse where they tended, as best they knew how, to his many wounds.

In the confusion of police, national police, government soldiers, ambulances, helicopters, dogs, and the press that had descended on the site, Bernardo had been put in a flatbed truck and moved to Juan's friend's house. The other man, the one staring back at him from the truck bed, was Felipe, who had in turn called Juan, who at the time was celebrating the good fortune he had received from Bernardo earlier in the morning. They decided to move him and keep him out of sight. No good Peruvians trusted anyone, and besides, this was a very wealthy one. Money could be made with such a move.

The truck was beginning to slow in the darkness, headlights off. The slight crescent of the moon lit the way. The rickety truck creaked and groaned, turning slowly to the right, and halted. Bernardo heard the slam of the truck doors, a squeaky gate being opened, and the truck moved forward again. It stopped once more while the gate was closed, chains clanking against steel posts, doors slamming again, and then an even rougher ride on what he guessed was an even more remote road. He managed to say a name, just before he passed out from the pain: "Emelia."

He awoke with a start, sitting upright, with terrible pain arching through his abdomen and arms. He was sweating profusely, and having a hard time catching his breath. A woman's face appeared in front of his. She was young, and had dark eyes and shiny skin that reflected from the artificial light in the warm room.

"Please, señor, please do not get up. You're badly injured. Lie back, please. You must not move." Her voice seemed urgent. She placed one arm behind his back, and used the other to gently push him back down onto the floor. His "bed" was a number of blankets that had been made into a pallet, with a sack of grain for a pillow. He was too weak to protest. She gently laid him back down again while his entire body protested with stabbing pain.

"Where....where am I?" His voice came out in a raspy whisper.

"You're safe. We have had the doctor here to see you. You're going to be all right, but you must rest. Juan is my older cousin. He has gone back to Ica to gather your belongings and bring them here. Please, señor, do not concern yourself right now. I'll give you something to help you rest…"

He watched the woman, almost helplessly, as she drew up a clear liquid into a syringe. He wanted to get up, but could barely speak.

"No…no…please don't give me anything." He felt as if he had exhausted any energy he had with the feeble protest.

"This will help with the pain, señor," she explained, and she stabbed the needle into his thigh, emptying the contents of the syringe. Warmth flowed through his body. He had the sensation of falling, and then—the squid ink of total unconsciousness flooded across his brain.

He awoke to daylight seeping through his eyelids. He placed his cupped hand over the top of his eyebrows to shield his eyes from the harsh sunlight. Pain coursed through his uplifted arm to his shoulder. Above him was a gray cement ceiling with a single light bulb hanging precariously from a fixture. It still hurt to breathe. He let his eyes roll to the right, and saw that he was in a small cement room. There was a propane stove with pots and pans hanging against the wall. Several large plastic buckets were near the stove. Thin clouds of smoke lay in the air. He turned his head to the left and saw the rest of wherever he was. There was a bed, covers pushed down towards the end, and a small battery-powered light on a stand, with a well-worn rug on the floor. Above the bed was a window, the source of the sunlight. He had no idea what time it was or where he was. A small dog in the corner perked up from his rest at Bernardo's movement. His tail wagged, and he gave out a sharp bark.

A noise turned his attention directly in front of him. A door opened, then slammed shut. It was the young woman who had drugged him. She smiled, and quickly moved towards him.

"Oh, señor. You're awake!" she said enthusiastically. "You have slept for several days. Let me get you some water." She took a cup from the nearby table and plunged it into one of the plastic buckets next to the stove, retrieving what appeared to be water, or old coffee, due to its pale brown color.

She placed the water next to him and helped him sit up. "Here, let me help you." Her strong arms lifted his torso to a sitting position. His ribs still hurt. His kidneys screamed for relief from the sitting position as he felt the air rush out of him.

"Ahhh," Bernardo sighed out in a long breath. She pulled the cup towards his lips, curling her arm behind his neck to help him.

"Here. Drink," she said.

He lifted a hand to help get the cup to his lips. The water tasted strongly of sulfur, but it was water nonetheless. Probably well water. No matter, it was cool, and wet. He drank the entire cupful.

"I have soup. I'll bring you some..." She padded barefoot to the stove, dipping a plastic bowl into the pot on the stove. Placing the soup on the bedside table, she gently pulled Bernardo to a more upright position, and pulled another grain bag behind his shoulders. Although it hurt, he had to admit he was feeling less pain than the last time he remembered. The woman held the steaming liquid under his mouth and slowly tipped it up.

"Drink this, señor, please."

The aroma smelled familiar to him. *Puchero*, he thought to himself. It smelled of beef, potatoes, and probably other vegetables and quinoa. He sipped the warm liquid. It tasted delicious. He sipped more.

"Slowly, señor. You have not eaten in many days. It will not stay down if you don't go slowly." She carefully withdrew the bowl from his lips.

"Thank you." His voice was weak, but sounded more like what he was used to.

"Where...." He started to ask a question, but she returned the bowl to his lips, and the smell of food overwhelmed his desire to talk.

"Let me do the talking, señor, and you eat. My name is Francesca. I have been caring for you while my husband, Felipe, and his cousin, Juan, the man that drove for you, went to Ica to get your things. It has not been easy. There are many police and soldiers investigating this explosion. They should be back this morning. They think you perished with the others. Is that true, señor?" She smiled at him, arching an eyebrow.

Bernardo shook his head to indicate no, and reached for more soup.

"They say the story has been all over the news on television and in the papers for the past few days. The Minister of Agriculture has been arrested in Lima, and several other members of some company…I can't remember the name."

"GMBI?" whispered Bernardo.

"Si, yes, that's the name. How did you know?" She looked at him as he continued to devour the soup.

"Lucky guess," Bernardo said quietly.

"Let me get you a spoon for the vegetables." She laid his head softly back down on the grain sack and walked to a plastic bucket, retrieving a plastic spoon with "McDonald's" emblazoned on the handle.

Bernardo took the spoon and began to eat the potatoes and vegetables left at the bottom of the bowl. They tasted wonderful.

"Francesca, do you have my cell phone anywhere?" He wondered what had been retrieved from his clothing, since the jogging pants and loose-fitting T-shirt he was wearing clearly were not his.

"Yes, I have it here, but you're very far in the country and there are no cell towers near here. There is no signal." She handed him the phone. It didn't matter anyway, since it was out of power. From the looks of where he was, there was little or no electricity, either. Besides, the charger he had in his briefcase had now become part of the atmosphere surrounding the large crater that was once a beautiful hacienda.

The dog that had been quietly resting near them suddenly perked up his ears and then ran towards the door, barking, but his tail was wagging. Far off in the distance, Bernardo heard the sound of a truck with bad exhaust manifolds coming towards them.

"Ahh. That must be Felipe and Juan now. I'll go look." She handed him the bowl and opened the door, letting more sunshine and fresh air into the room. The truck noise grew louder, and finally ceased into squeaking brakes. Doors opened and slammed shut, the dog barked a happy bark, and voices joined together in welcomes, descriptions of the adventure, and laughter.

A head peered through the doorway. It was Juan.

"Ahhh, señor, you're back with us! This is very good. We were worried about you; but I see Francesca has brought you back to life, eh?" He laughed and moved towards Bernardo, lowering his voice.

"Señor, we were able to sneak into your room last night and get your belongings. There were police all over, but most of them were drunk by midnight. We snuck in through the balcony window and packed your belongings and brought them here. Shall I bring them in?"

"Yes, please." Bernardo struggled to get up.

"No, no, señor. Stay still, please. You have been badly hurt. It will be a few more days before you can move about. Stay still, please. I'll bring in your bags. Oh, yes, and I have another surprise for you. I'll bring that in, too."

Bernardo couldn't imagine what Juan was talking about. He disappeared through the door, and a moment later, he and Felipe were carrying two suitcases in and placing them near his bed. He heard women's voices behind them. Francesca walked in first, with a big smile on her face, and then another woman followed her into the room. It was Emelia. He felt as if his heart had stopped beating, staring at her beautiful face.

"My God!" was all he could muster, and then the room colored inky black with unconsciousness.

Chapter Twenty-Seven - Emelia

Bernardo felt warmth all over his body. He was dreaming. He knew, even though it was impossible, that his wife was with him now. It was such a vivid dream. He could smell her perfume. Maybe he was dead. No matter, he knew he was with her, perhaps now forever. He felt himself being lifted up by many hands. He was floating. Then cool cotton sheets that smelled of soap enveloped him. He didn't want to open his eyes, but he did. He was staring at brown wooden beams contrasted against a white ceiling. He looked to his right. Emelia's face shone as their eyes met. Yes, he knew he had to be in heaven. It was nice, he thought. Being dead isn't so bad. He reached up towards Emelia's face with his right arm and felt pain coursing through to his shoulder. Pain?

"Emelia, my darling; is it really you? Where are we? What…I don't…how…" his thoughts were overwhelming his ability to speak.

"Yes, it's me, my love." Emelia touched his cheek. "We're in Cuzco, in our Nido de Búho. You're safe. *We're* safe now. No one will be bothering us any longer, you certainly saw to that. In fact, we're both officially dead!" She laughed. "So, welcome to the afterlife!" she joked, laughing softly. "When you're completely well, we must consider what to do next. I hear America needs some help; perhaps we can go to live there." Emelia curled up next to her husband, pulling an alpaca throw over the two of them, and Bernardo closed his eyes, finding the rest and peace that had evaded him in the past weeks. *Thank you, Pachamama*, he thought to himself, and fell into a deep sleep.

THE END

Epilogue

The day of the massive explosion in Ica, several newspapers and television stations in Lima had a second big story to cover; the first, of course, had been the earthquake. Even as the people in Lima had been digging out of the rubble, the military had acted swiftly to arrest the Minister of Agriculture, and a host of staff members that were involved in the conspiracy with GMBI. The president of GMBI himself had disavowed any knowledge of this plan, claiming instead that the R&D department had acted alone in this insane and insidious plot to control food in the country of Peru... Nevertheless, GMBI's headquarters in Lima were shut down, and the company's presence evaporated like the early morning fog from the Pacific. Services were held for a large number of powerful dignitaries and officials killed in the blast in Ica. Mourners especially paid tribute to

Bernardo Villacorta and his wife, Emelia, who were interred outside their home in Ancón, an enormous hacienda that had been left to Juan Arturo Velasquez, a former driver of Sr. Villacorta.

About the Author

John Massey inherited his love for books from his father, a career English teacher in the New York City Public Schools. He committed to his father—who passed away at age ninety-one—he would finish his dream of writing and publishing a novel. Massey received his bachelor's degree in English literature from the University of Cincinnati, also earning a master's degree there.

This first novel represents Massey's admiration and love of the people of Peru through images of the Peruvian and Incan culture, past and present. He and his wife, Judy, traveled there numerous times over the years. They reside in Boca Raton, Florida, with their Bichon, Zoe Neige. Massey has three children—Alison, David, and Caroline.